I0683795

FRIEND

OF

THE FAMILY

By: G. Legacy

Chapter 1

The headboard swayed and rocked into the wall. The creek of bedrails struggling to remain latched joined the symphony of warped and whining boards, beneath wiry coils in the box spring to form a syncopated rhythm of lust.

Bombed from above. Her vaginal canal invaded by nine-inch thrust, piercing, parting and plowing until their pelvis became one. The impact absorbed by the mattress caused it to take the shape of its impressionist, a large shapely ass that clenched and clapped in applause. Giving praise to the performance of his apparatus.

"Mnnnn!" Her nails found their way beneath the skins surface. "Mnn … Mnnn … Oooh!"

Scraping small strips of flesh from his back as he shoved himself deeper and deeper inside.

He looked down staring into her eyes. "That's right." His expression that of a surgeon performing a complicated procedure.

She was unsure. Was he referring to her moans, or the flagellating sputter of her labia fluttering and flapping with joy, expressing the delight she felt in the pit of her loins.

"Oh God!" Why was she calling upon the one being, whom decreed such feelings of lust a sin? "Oh God. That feels so good!"

His shoulders flexed and bowed, head tilting into her bosom, hips moving much quicker now she was once again granted the option to squeal and squirm, releasing knots of tension by way of orgasm after orgasm.

"Ooooooohh!"

But it wasn't over. His manhood stood tall in the ambience of her velvet interior, refusing to lose posture, saluting the walls of desire when suddenly he yanked himself away.

Her corridors of yearning collapsed upon departure, lips colliding with an audible kiss. Sputtering once more, as he swung her leg over the opposite hip, sending her rolling onto her stomach.

Grabbing her from behind his thumbs pressed and spread her cheeks. Angling her in a downward dog position he stood on the bed, taking a low crouch he aimed his rigid spear at its target and sumo squatted his way inside once again.

"Awwhh!" She squawked.

Grabbing the sheets attempting to pull herself away from the dangling rails descent, she only managed to peel them from the mattress, pulling them into a fist filled bundle which she shoved into her mouth, screaming into the new found gag like a hostage begging to be freed.

But tonight there was no ransom. No kidnappers. Just him. There was no price to be paid for emancipation, only his mercy would suffice. Though at the moment it appeared this would not be taken into consideration.

"Chavis!" His name wrestled from her tongue between gasps and teeth grinding expletives.

Chavis reached forward, fingers wide-spread forming a halo before becoming a crown that clutched her skull, tilting her head back so that she came from elbows to an upright kneel.

"Chavis!" She called out again.

"Evelyn!" His tone laced with sarcasm.

It was clear he didn't feel sorry for her. He never did. This is what she asked for, he always reminded, and he was right, she did. Every time she chose to present herself before him sauntering about in revealing skirts. Taking no more than a slight bend or squat to reveal peeks at the cupps of her ass and the pouty mound beneath her panties. Whenever she chose to wear any.

Tonight she had not. She'd taken them off in the car. Sliding them down her thighs. Slipping them over her stiletto heels, over her toes, leaving them to rest on the floorboard, where they still lay draped across the gas pedal.

The car sat outside, unoccupied, just as she'd left it when teetering from the automobile earlier, tipsy from one too many sips of champagne she'd made her way to his door, stumbling up the steps, scrambling for the doorbell she awakened him in the wee hours of the night. Meeting him at the door with hunger filled tugs at his boxer briefs and pleading kisses all over his lips, neck and chest.

Like always he'd received her with open arms. Her feet leaving the floor, legs around his waist, carried to the bedroom where the full on assault instantaneously began.

No. There was no need for her to whine, now. No need for her to cry, but the realization did nothing to stop her eyes from tearing up, trickling from tight squinted lids, rolling down the sides of her cheeks. Mourning fidelity's death while celebrating a moment that felt like a lifetime condensed and compiled in the confines of her mind, spirit and nether-regions all in one instance.

"Oooohh!" She vibrated inside.

Falling from her knees to her stomach, the hitch attaching them bringing him down upon her, she felt herself dissolve into the bed's surface, spreading across the king-size mattress in a pit of sweat and goo.

"Mnnnmnn!" She was numb. "Mnnnnn." Drunk.

Pounded to inebriation by sledge hammering blows that made her backside wobble, and toes spread as if trying to part ways with the balls of her feet, till finally his rod began to fluctuate. Morphing to a swell the shaft enlarged for a split-second then recoiled upon release, spewing thick pearls from its head into her womb. Tainting it with spillage that would be foreign to her husband's tongue.

That is If she were to find the urge to welcome herself home in such a way, whenever she decided to get dressed and make her way to their house, their bed, to him. The one she'd given vows to.

Chavis stretched out inside her. Emptying his hose completely before dragging it away from her, one inch at a time, savoring the warmth of her cradle along the way till finally making an exit.

Leaving a resin trail, a slimy zig-zag line down the length of her thigh as he rolled off her onto his back.

Evelyn next to him, upper-lip curled, tongue hanging from her mouth found the strength to speak. "I gotta go."

Chavis got up. Using his hand to palm away a bit of left over sludge he smacked her on the ass, leaving a damp palm print behind as he went to the bathroom to take a piss.

The sound of urine splattering against the commode was overshadowed by the sound of his voice calling out to Evelyn as she crawled from the bed, slipped on her shoes and pulled her dress over her head.

"Lock the door on your way out!"

And without another word between them, she did just that.

Chapter 2

The bright sun pouring through the curtains, accompanied by his girlfriend's voice brought Aaron's eyes to life.

"Rise and shine." Kaleico smiled at her man, thumbing her tongue she wiped at the corner of his eye.

"Stop girl!" He hated when she groomed him like a child, or a pet. "Get off me, you're …"

He realized something was ary. Either he'd awakened from a wet dream, or his genitals were wet, for   very wide awake reasons.

Kaleico biting her lower lip blushed with embarrassment. "What?" She giggled. "I was horny!" She made the walls of her vagina flex. "Sue me!"

His manhood compressed as her vulva clenched then released. Not only had he not realized he was inside her, he noticed for the first time her banana like breast were perky and free of restrictive garments.

Last night when he'd come from work, she was already in a fetal position full pajamas, snoring lightly, eyes behind a bedtime mask. Now here she was on top of him ass naked.

His groggy mood suddenly changed. "Well good morning to you!"

She gave her hips a slow, forward roll. "Oh, now you all jubilant, all of a sudden?"

He grabbed her waist and arched his pelvis. "Can you blame me?"

Mmmmn ... I ... Mnnn ... I can't say that I can ... Mnnmmnn."

Their movements became more eager. kaleico sucked air through clenched teeth, leaning forward so the tips of their noses touched, they worked in accord to reach a mutual goal.

Their genitals filled the quiet bedroom with osculating sounds, similar to a starving man slurping and smacking away at a long awaited bowl of soup and noodles.

"Mnhh ..." She moaned again, when the alarm clock began to blare. "Nmhh!"

Placing one hand on his chest she slapped the snooze button with her free hand.

"Mhhnn!"

It was time for them to get up, to prepare for their flight. They were due at the airport soon.

"Okay." She purred. "Mnn...Okay … Ohmm... We gotta hurr... Mnnh... Come on... Mnn...Come o…Mnhh… Come on. Come on. Come … Ahmph!"

His toes rolled into knots as she chased an orgasm, using him as the means and mode of transport to give chase. He did all he could to hold back the urge to explode with each jerk of the hips.

"Ohh... okay...mnn...ohhh...ohhh … ohhhh … ohhhhh!" She quaked.

"Shit!" He let loose inside her, as she released all over his pulsing flesh.

Collapsing on top of him. She kissed him on the nose then the lips.

Perking up she gave him another peck. "Okay." Rolling to a full stance her bare feet hit the carpet. "Come on."

Looking over her shoulder as she walked towards the bathroom. "Get dressed. We have a plane to catch!"

He called after her. "Mile high club?"

"It's not Christmas yet, buddy!" She disappeared into the bathroom.

"Close enough!"

He could hear the shower turn on, her voice echoing a reply. "Tell me what you got me and it's a deal."

Rolling out of bed he laughed to himself, there was no way he was gonna reveal the Christmas surprise before it's time. "Not a chance! Guess I'll have to anticipate in the sky, what I'm guaranteed to get once we touch land again."

"Boy. My momma will kill you and me, both if we even think about laying a lustful hand on one another, under her roof!"

She listened for a remark as she lathered herself. There was no reply. He'd already left the bedroom, choosing to shower downstairs. Knowing if he were to shower with her, they would never get to the airport on time. There was no way he'd be the reason for a late arrival

11

to her home town for the holidays. That would make a terrible first impression on her family.

Hopping in the shower he turned the knob and prepared for the journey ahead.

"Charlotte, North Carolina. Here we come!"

Chapter 3

"Ma. How come Kaleico get all this special treatment?" Kaleico's younger sister, Zayeda asked.

Their mother, Sandra looked at her with a glare remnant of a librarians, right before the "shush."

Sandra turned her gaze back to the steaming pot in front of her. Placing the lid over it, wiping her hands on her apron, before opening the oven to check the cornbread.

Zayeda, "Zee" as they called her, continued. "I'm just saying. Everybody act like she the golden child or something. It's not even Christmas yet, but it look like you're cooking a Christmas dinner." She stood by the counter opposite her mother. "And you only doing it cause she's coming!"

"Zayeda. Get outta here bothering me!" She closed the oven and faced her. "Yes. I am happy that my first born is the first of many in our family to attend college." She wiped her brow

13

and fanned herself. "You notice I said 'first' cause in a few years you will be on your way to do the same."

Zayeda flipped her hair, wanting no parts of the college discussion she turned to leave the kitchen.

Sandra yelled behind her. "And go put on some clothes! Walking around with those little ass shorts on!"

Zayeda sauntered up the stairs. Plucking the hem of her shorts from her rear. Each step making them ride up her crotch till she reached the top, heading for her bedroom.

Wrestling a finger in her pocket she fished out a small key. The sign on her door-Stay Out-wasn't enough to keep her mother away these days. She'd opted for a lock and key to aid in her battle for privacy.

The door opened and everything she loved about life welcomed her to the room. Her laptop sat open on the desk, the screen saver a large bouncing Emoji in her own image, with the words 'you're beautiful' overhead illuminating the room. A familiar buzz from her dresser let her know that someone was texting her.

She caught the phone just as it vibrated towards the edge, about to fall off and hit the floor. Good thing she had nice fluffy carpet, wasn't too often she caught it before it fell.

Checking the message she rolled her eyes and replied with a few prods and pokes then tossed the phone on the bed.

Peeling her shorts off she mocked "Take those shorts off" and tossed them before walking towards the closet.

After a moment she emerged with a pair of jeans in her grips. Moving to the bed she sat on the edge and slipped her feet through the legs, pulling them as high as the knee before getting stuck. Improvising she slid off the bed towards the floor, pulling on the waistline all the while, till she managed to get them just beneath her cheeks.

"Dag. My butt getting big!" She giggled.

Holding the waistband she began to jump up and down, yanking on them at the same time.

Finally. Problem was, now the shirt no longer matched. A tank top would do. She wasn't going outside and if she did decide to, it was nothing a jacket couldn't fix.

Satisfied. Plopping on her bed, laying back on the pillow the back of her noggin began to vibrate. Reaching under the pillow she grabbed the phone, holding it towards the ceiling with a smile on her face as an image appeared on the screen.

Male genitalia, dangling from a torso with no face visible. The message beneath it reading. FOR YOU.

About to reply, a ruckus from downstairs caught her ear stealing her attention. Clearing the screen, pushing the phone back under the pillow Zayeda jumped to her feet and left the room. There was no doubt in her mind what the cause of all the commotion was.

.....

Kaleico stood at the mailbox, taking it all in. Even from outside home was all she remembered it to be. Her mother's cornbread creeping into the front drive had welcomed her when she stepped out of the cab. The fragrance was all too familiar. Just the right amount of sweet: Nostalgia in every bite. She couldn't wait.

A quick trot and a skip, leaving Aaron at the edge of the drive, with both of their luggage at his feet, she was already knocking before realizing what she had done.

"Oh." She ran back to him, grabbing one of the bags from the ground. Tugging him and the luggage he toted hurridly back to the door, just before it opened.

·····

"My baby!" Sandra cried. "My sweet, sweet baby!"

Kaleico's mother strangled her with love. Aaron stood just inside the doorway, watching as she pulled Kaleico inside and gushed over her, taking pause only long enough to peer over her shoulder, giving him the once over.

Sandra pushed Kaleico aside. "My. My. My." Extending both arms. "Aren't you handsome!"

Kaleico stood behind her as Sandra began to hug and gush over Aaron as well. Aaron looked over her shoulder at Kaleico, his smile turning to a straight line, eyes bulging suddenly.

"Ooh." Sandra coo'd "And he's got such a nice ass."

"Ma!" Kaleico grabbed her mother pulling her away. "Hands off!"

Aaron's face was flush. He didn't know what to say.

Kaleico helped him "Don't worry. She just likes to tease." She faced Sandra. "Dag, Ma. We been here thirty seconds and you already scaring him!"

Sandra chuckled then hugged her first born yet again. "Oh baby, I'm so glad you're home. So, so happy you're here." Turning to Aaron again. "Don't just stand there sweety. Throw those bags in the corner and make yourself comfy."

"Yes mam." Doing as told, placing the bags by the wall. "Umm. Mam, may I use your restroom?"

"Only if you stop calling me Mam!" She waved the gesture off. "It's, Sandra, sweetheart." She pointed. "That way, to the right."

Following her direction he headed for the bathroom. Coming upon a stairway along the way he bumped into Zayeda as she hopped down over the last two steps.

"Oh!" She stopped. "I'm sorry!" She looked him over. "You must be the new boyfriend!"

"That would be him." Kaleico called out. "Hey little sis."

Zayeda was curt. "Hey." Turning back to Aaron extending a hand. "Nice to meet you." She shook his hand and ran back up the steps.

Kaleico looked to Sandra who only waved dismissively.

Sandra reminded. "I'm sure you remember when you first started smelling yourself. You know how it is."

Calico gasped. "I was never like, that."

They shared a laugh while Aaron stayed the course to the restroom. Kaleico's voice a distant muffle once he stepped in and closed the door.

"Speaking of smelling" she said. "Where's the cornbread?"

Chapter 4

Zayeda lay in bed, phone in hand, selecting an Emoji- A frowny face before pressing send.

Seconds later a reply "What's wrong? Why so sad?"

Her answer was short. "My sister's home. SMH. Attention whore!" pressing send she added as an afterthought "Nobody sees me when she's around." Send.

A rap at the door interrupted. She slid the phone under the pillow, ignoring the incoming reply she went to the door. It was Kaleico.

"Hey." Kaleico spoke through the crack. "Can I come in?"

Zayeda exhaled and returned to her bed as Kaleico entered.

Kaleico looked around. Everything was different. "Wow!" She ran her fingers over a poster on the wall. A rap group. Next to it an R&B star. "You've really settled in. Made it your own. It's nice."

Zayeda lay on her side, face nestled in the pillow, indifferent. "No one was using it. So why not?"

"No. I mean, why not? It's bigger than your old room. More space. I was just saying it's nice, that's all."

"It's okay, I guess."

Kaleico looked towards the window. Walking over she grabbed the curtains. "Except for the crappy ..." she opened them. "View."

The privacy fence. It was gone. She could see clear from their backyard to the neighboring house behind them, one block over, backyards connecting. She was shocked.

Zayeda sat upright. "That fence is long gone." She said. "If you came around sometimes you'ld know that."

Kaleico started to reply but Zayeda didn't allow her a word in between.

"Is mom done cooking?" Not waiting for an answer she sprung from the bed and left the room.

Kaleico stood there alone. Her sister was clearly pissed about something. What or why she had no clue, she turned to close the curtains when she saw a light, in the upstairs window of the house behind them. A shadow appeared and the blinds opened.

There was a silhouette behind the blinds. Then the blinds began to rise completely, revealing the figure behind them. Looking at the windows inhabitant, all Kaleico could do was smile, from ear to ear.

.....

Chavis looked at his phone. Evelyn's name flashed on the screen. "Hello."

She was horny. It was earlier than usual. The sun had barely made an exit. She wasn't even drunk, leaving no room for her usual excuse for cravings of infidelity.

Chavis listened. She was irritating him "come on, Evelyn. You know the rules. Way too short notice. Beside's." He walked to the bedroom window. "I'm about to do something else right now. How bout we just do it lat ..." he paused when he peeped between the blinds.

He spread them wider to get a better look.

"Matter of fact ..." He pulled the blind up completely. "Let ... Let me call you back."

He hung up, despite her protest. He couldn't believe it. A broad smile crossed his face as he waved hello.

Across the backyard in the window of the house behind him, she waved back. Even from so far away, her smile as bright as ever.

"Kaleico." He uttered to himself. "She's home."

Chapter 5

Kaleico ran downstairs. Her mother was setting the table. Aaron and Zayeda sat across from one another, engaged in conversation.

"Ma!" Kaleico exclaimed. "You didn't tell me Cha.."

The phone on the wall rang. Her mother grabbed it and looked at the caller I.D.

"It's for you." She passed Kaleico the phone without answering. "Tell him I just cooked. If he's hungry he's welcome to join us." Sandra looked to Aaron and mouthed. "Childhood friend."

"Oh." Aaron smiled.

Zayeda specified. "Chavis."

Zayeda smirked, looking to Aaron who looked to Kaleico, so caught up in her conversation she noticed none of it.

"Oh." Aaron's tone shifted.

Kaleico smiled at the phone. "Okay. I'll tell her. Love you too. Bye!"

Sandra slapped Aaron's shoulder giving him reassurance. "Not that kind of love."

Before Aaron replied Kaleico cut in. "Ma. He knows that." She walked over and gave him a peck on the cheek. "Aaron knows he's the only
24

man for me." She pulled a chair up next to him. "Chavis is a very close friend. Like a brother, almost."

Sandra on the sideline nodded.

Kaleico examined Aaron a moment. "You weren't about to get jealous, were you?"

"No!" Aaron denied.

Kaleico put an elbow on the table placing a fist under her chin for a prop.

She looked him in the eyes. "So what are you saying? I'm not worth getting jealous over?"

"No!"

Sandra and Kaleico enjoyed his bumbling. Zayeda got up from the table.

Speaking over her shoulder adding her two cents as she left. "Please tell her yes. She oh, so enjoys the attention!"

There was an awkward silence as she jetted up the steps, going back to her room. Kaleico shook her head then reached for the plate in the center of the table, grabbing a square of cornbread.

Biting a piece off she then held it to Aaron's mouth. "Taste it. You're gonna love it!"

"Careful!" Sandra warned. "You know that cornbread snagged me your daddy, back in the days." She winked at Aaron. "Then again, it is getting kind of lonely around here. Go ahead and give him a bite!"

. . . . .

Chavis stood peering out of the window. Remembering a time when this very window once allowed a view of the in-ground swimming pool in Kaleico's backyard. But that was before the fence came. Then after the fence came tragedy. After that everything changed.

The fence was gone now. He looked at the green grass that covered every inch of Sandra's backyard. The same backyard he once watched Kaleico swim and play in for hours. The pool, like the fence, was gone now. Filled in with dirt, covered with seed leaving behind grass and nothing more.

So much had changed. Chavis turned to the mirror. A dark scar on his chest called to his fingertips, begging to be touched. He rubbed the scar. A constant reminder that some things never changed at all.

None. What so ever.

His phone began to ring. Her again. Evelyn.

"Hello … Evelyn, I already told you once. Not tonight … Tomorrow maybe." He hung up.

Taking one last look out the window before grabbing his keys, heading for the garage he got in his car and left the house.

Chapter 6

"This is where you'll be sleeping." Sandra flipped the light switch on.

Aaron looked at the small bed. Power Puff Girls in an array of fight poses covered the quilt, matching perfectly with the images on the wall runners and curtains.

Sandra smirked. "Just enough bed for one!" She pulled Kaleico, standing just outside the door, over the threshold holding her close. "Don't worry. There's room for your girlfriend, my sweet daughter, in my bed!"

"Ma!"

"Unless." Sandra now addressed Kaleico. "You wanna share a room with your sister?"

Kaleico poked her lip out.

Sandra looked back to Aaron, also clearly disappointed. "I'm sure you understand, son?" She explained. "No sharing a room under my roof till after vows have been made and honeymoons have been had!"

She pulled Kaleico's arm. Kaleico resisted long enough to wave Aaron over for a peck on the lips.

"Goodnight." She told him.

Sandra tugged harder. "Nighty night! We'll be upstairs if you need us." She added. "If you get any late night cravings, the fridge is open. Help yourself! Goodniiight!"

She sang as she pulled Kaleico up the steps.

Chapter 7

Kaleico stood in front of the mirror. The image staring back at her was a tiny little girl. The girl was 10 years old. Kaleico knew this because right next to the full length mirror, mounted on the closet door, there were etched markings on the wall that measured her height, with her age scratched right next to it.

She touched the etching. The line was a deep groove carved by her father with a hawk billed knife he used when fishing. Looking up she could see more lines. Too far for her tiny arms to reach. 13 years. 14 years. 15 years. 16 years. How could they be so out of reach? Hadn't she lived to see them all pass already? Why was she so small?

It's a dream sweety. It's a dream. A distant thought, or was it a voice? That's it. It was a voice. Distorted at first. Low and deep. Devilish almost. Then the voice became clear. A familiar tone. Strong. Husky. Gentle.

"You're having a dream, sweety." Her father appeared behind her in the mirror. His knee just above her chin.

He was a tall man. Big and strong. She wished for him to lift her in his strong arms and toss her into the air. Reaching for his hands she pointed towards the lines etched high overhead. She didn't want to be a little girl. Wanted to be taller. Older.

"Pick me up, daddy." She pleaded.

He didn't budge. Only looked down at her and smiled.

"Pick me up, daddy."

Nothing.

"Pick me up. Please!" She whimpered. "Please!"

Wanting to be higher. Needing to be older. She wanted to touch the line marked 16. The last line his hawk billed blade ever etched. A thing he'd still taken joy in, even as she'd become a teen. Even if she'd failed to grow as much as another inch. He'd always mark her spot. Right next to it her age and date. Even if it meant cutting a deeper groove in the same spot he'd carved the year before.

"Please daddy. I wanna be right here." Her little eyes tearing up she looked anxiously at the deep groove. The number 16 carved next to it. "I wanna be 16 again. I wanna be 16 again. Daddy please! Please daddy! Please!"

"Shhhh." The voice echoed as her father stood silent. "You're dreaming. It's just a dream. You're just having a bad, bad dream."

.....

"UnGH!" Aaron jerked, knocking the covers off the bed. "Wh… unh?"

He looked around. Realizing he'd been awakened by a sound overhead, a light thud, shuffling of feet and a low scrape, more footsteps, then what sounded like the creak of worn bedsprings. A singular creak. Someone plopping onto the bed no doubt.

His eyes scanned the ceiling, tracing their way to the source of the sound. A vent tucked above the headboard right where the ceiling and the wall connected.

The sounds had traveled through the air duct, from the room above. He looked at the vent, listening. Nothing. A sound from outside took his attention, getting to his feet he walked to the window. The window faced the street, the curtains were closed but he could see two specs of light in the distance. Taillights.

A low clunk followed as he spread the curtains, by the time they were open the lights were getting smaller, the car disappearing around the corner.

Dogs barked in the distance. The night air pressed frost against the glass pane as he wiped the dew from the inside and tried to get a clear view of what was outside. Nothing. The air from his nostrils only made the windows fog all the more.

Closing the curtains he stepped back towards the bed. Pausing he scratched himself and decided the bathroom was too far away. Hopefully he wouldn't piss on himself.

Exhausted from the flight he decided moving any further was out of the question, retrieving the blanket from the floor he threw it, and himself back on the bed. His bladder would have to wait. Right now all he wanted was to pull the covers over his head and get some rest.

Chapter 8

The tip of his manhood tingled. Tickled by moisture that caused pressure to build in his loins. Fearing he was about to wet himself Aaron made a groggy attempt to roll out of bed, but his legs were pinned down.

His eyes barely open, he looked to see why his legs weren't moving. Kaleico lay with her forearms resting on his thighs, a grin on her face looking up at him as she held his shaft in her hand, blowing on the head, teasingly.

"Kaleico." He nudged her nervously. "Your mom, what are you do.." he leapt from the bed, tucking his privates back inside his pajamas. 'You trying to get me killed up in here?" He whispered.

Walking to the door he peeked out into the hall.

"Boy. My momma in the kitchen making breakfast."

She got up and trailed behind him. "I was just messing with your scary ass." She pinched his rear.

"Stop girl."

She giggled. "Where you going?"

"To the bathroom. I been holding it all night."

Grabbing him from behind she bit him between the shoulder blades and muffled. "Well hurry up. Breakfast is almost done. I just wanted to wake you up."

He stepped into the hall and made a quick sprint to the restroom. Upon his return he entered the bedroom and found Kaleico standing on the bed, leaning on the wall by the headboard she looked up and chanted. "Wake up sleepy head. Wake up! Waake uuuup!"

The vent overhead replied. "Kaleico. Shut up!"

Zayeda's voice conveyed that she clearly was not in the mood to be disturbed.

"Fine!" Kaleico shot back. "Suit yourself!"

Aaron looked at her as she flipped a middle finger at the vent then stepped down off the bed.

Walking by him she gave him a peck on the lips. "Brush your teeth. I'm about to go fix you a plate." She stopped and added. "Will it be blueberry or chocolate chip?"

"Wow. I get to choose?" He began to tease. "You better be careful. Your mom keep spoiling me like this, you just might be returning home alone."

"Cute." She smiled. "The shower is upstairs to the left. The hot water tends to go on the fritz. So don't be surprised if you go in like this." She held up a fist. "And come out like this." She wiggled a pinky then closed the door before he could reply.

·····

Just as promised the water had taken a sudden chill, signaling it was time to bring the shower to an end.

Stepping out onto the fluffy carpet laying flush against the tub, Aaron gave himself a shake and used his palms to brush away any excess water before toweling himself dry.

Stepping into his sweats, he lotioned his upper body, threw the towel over his shoulder and hustled down the staircase. Stopping by the room he slept in, long enough to toss his things and put on a shirt, he then followed his nostrils to the kitchen.

Bending the corner he could hear the clatter of forks and plates amidst giddy chatter. No doubt Kaleico and her mother were enjoying their time together. Entering the kitchen he realized it was not only Kaleico's mother who enjoyed her company.

Kaleico was the first to notice him. Aaron's eyes met hers then traveled to her mother, quickly moving to the well chiseled male that sat between them.

Kaleico stood. "Hey baby." Meeting him at the threshold pulling him towards the table. "I have someone I want you to meet."

"So!" Chavis stood "This is Aaron." Extending a hand.

Aaron met his palm with his own. He noticed how strong his grip was immediately.

Chavis was slender and taut, with broad shoulders and forearms like a pro Baseball player.

Aaron struggled. "And you must be …"

"Chavis."

"Ahh. Yes." Aaron nodded. "I've heard a lot about you."

"Yeah? Well," Chavis held firm, yet to release his hand. "I guess I can say I've heard a lot about you, too." He looked at Kaleico and shrugged. "As much as one can hear in the past ten minutes, I suppose."

There was an awkward pause. Their grips loosened and Chavis took his spot back at the table.

Grabbing a fork he took a bite from the pancakes in front of him and gestured to a plate at the end of the table. "You really gotta try these. Sandra makes the best cakes!" He took another bite. "Pancakes, cupcakes, upside-down cakes. You name it!"

Sandra blushed. "He just loves to flatter an old lady, that's all."

She tapped him on the shoulder. Aaron laughed at the exchange. Kaleico urged him with her eyes to have a seat as she returned to her initial spot.

Aaron took a seat in front of the awaiting plate of pancakes. "Smells good."

"Thanks." Sandra smiled. Getting up from her seat, stepping around Chavis and Kaleico to get to Aaron. "Pick your poison!" She grabbed two decorative flask of syrup.

Aaron look at them one dark, the other light in color. "Whatever the lady suggests."

"The house special it is!" Sandra tilted them both over his plate, creating a blended drizzle that oozed all over the cakes.

"Okay, Ma!" Kaleico reached over taking the syrup from her hand. "That's quite enough." Shooing Sandra back to her seat. "You trying to give my man high cholesterol?"

Chavis took a strip of bacon in his grip, snapping a bite off. "Dog, Kaleico. Let the man live a little." He pointed with the bacon. "You acting like a little syrup gonna kill him." Facing Aaron. "Tell her, you're a man not one of those, what they call em? .. Metrosexuals."

Chavis chuckled then realized he was the only one laughing.

He looked for confirmation. "I mean, you're not, right?"

Aaron laughed. "Nah. Of course no..."

"Hey, Chavis." Zayeda appeared from nowhere, walking over to give him a hug, reaching across his chest to grab a slice of bacon from his plate.

Chavis pretended to stab at her finger with the fork.

Sandra laughed at them then looked to Aaron. "I don't know what I'd do around here without those two to keep me company." She clasped Chavis' hand. "Especially this one. I swear, I call him at least once a week to fix something around here."

Chavis was humble. "Any excuse to feed me." He took another bite. "I live in that big ol' house of mine, alone. She feels sorry for me.

Kaleico joked. "Good job with the shower, by the way!"

Chavis nudged her on the chin. "Ha ha ha!" He mocked. "She said, I was always on hand, not the handiest man!"

Sandra giggled, speaking in his defense. "Well. It used to stay hot for only two minutes. Now it's..."

"Five." Aaron interjected. Picking up the syrup, drizzling more on his pancakes.

This time it was he who took the bacon, snapping a piece off between clenched teeth.

Pointing what remained of it towards Chavis. "So. You been living around here for a while, huh?"

"All my life."

Aaron nodded. "Well, from what Kaleico has told me, her father was very protective. So I'm sure he'd be glad to know his girls are being watched over." He gestured to Sandra and Zayeda, who stood by the fridge drinking from a jug of orange juice.

Everyone froze and quieted at the mention of Kaleico's father, Sandra's deceased husband.

Kaleico seeing her mother rise slowly from the table reached for her. "Ma ..."

Chavis did the same. "Sandra."

Sandra pulled away. "Well, maybe if he would've stayed around to watch us his self ..."

"Ma." Kaleico grabbed her hand.

She pulled away again, this time with a look of grief on her face.

42

Chavis cleared his throat, distracting from the awkward moment. "So, tell me Aaron. What does a guy like yourself like to do for fun?"

Aaron had no clue what he'd done wrong but was glad for the chance to draw attention from the foot in his mouth.

He shrugged. "I don't know? Some of everything I guess. If it's fun to do, I like to do it, I suppose."

"Alright." Chavis made it final. "I guess that means the ladies will have to find something to do amidst themselves today." He held up his glass of orange juice. "Me and my man, Aaron here gonna go see what we can get into."

He looked to Kaleico who looked to Aaron and smiled. A smile Aaron returned reluctantly, when suddenly the sound of a car door shutting outside stole the moment.

The sound of a familiar voice looming outside made Kaleico's face come aglow.

"Where's my favorite cousin! Where she at! Where she at!" The voice got louder.

"Lawd have mercy." Kaleico looked to her mother who seemed to brighten as well. "I see, she's still loud."

Sandra assured her. "Loud and more annoying than ever!"

Her cousin, Chantelle, screamed through the front door as she rang the doorbell repeatedly. "Kaleico!"

Kaleico jumped from the table and ran through the living room to the door, leaving the others in the kitchen, craning their necks.

Sandra spoke. "That girl know good and well it's too early in the morning for all that noise."

"Here I am!" Kaleico chimed as she swung the door open.

Chantelle, her first cousin, the same age as herself, leapt into her arms and squeezed tight, "Girl, I miss you! You know as soon as my momma told me that you was here, I was like unuh! Yall better get up out that bed and get me over there to see my girl!"

Kaleico hugged her back then held her at a distance. "Wow! Where did those come from?"

Chantelle stepped back and lift her breast, pushing them together. "Well. I guess you can say, I went out one day to cop a new wig and next thing you know, I come home with new ta-ta's instead!"

"Girl, you are a mess." Kaleico examined them. "I must say, they do look nice, though." She felt them. "Feel nice too!"

"That's what *he* said!" Chantelle quipped.

"You mean, they!" Kaleico joked.

"Well" Chantelle flipped her hair. "You know."

They were so caught up in their own babble they failed to realize they were blocking the doorway.

Chantelle turned around. "Oh. Daddy, I'm sorry!"

Kaleico looked over Chantelle's shoulder. "Oh. Hey Uncle Mel!"

Her Uncle Melvin sat, gazing up at her from his wheelchair, and behind him Sandra's sister-Kaleico's Aunt stood grimacing at Chantelle.

"Chantelle. Can you stop yappin long enough for me to help your daddy inside?"

"I'm sorry, Ma." Chantelle stepped inside the living room so they could enter, when she suddenly noticed there was an unfamiliar face in the kitchen. "Well, who is this?"

She pushed Kaleico aside and walked towards Aaron. Zayeda rolled her eyes, as

Chantelle extended her wrist as if expecting it to be kissed. "My name is Chantelle, and you are?"

Kaleico yelled from the other room. "He is my damn man! Get away from him and leave him alone."

"Don't nobody want your man!" She still held her wrist out.

Aaron shook her hand.

"She got you trained, ain't she?" Chantelle poked then greeted everyone else at the table.

Zayeda gave her a reluctant hug. Aaron got a kiss on the cheek.

"Hey, Aunt Sandra."

"Hey, crazy."

Kaleico, still in the living room, gave her Uncle Melvin a hug. He just stared, in a daze while her Aunt turned to close the door then removed her coat.

Kaleico took her coat, giving her a one armed hug. "I see you're still looking as youthful as ever." She stepped away to hang the coat. "And your daughter is still crazy!"

"Crazy ain't the word." She pushed Melvin towards the kitchen, Kaleico followed. "You need to get her outta my house and take her with you.

Out here running round with tuition money on her chest!"

She brought her husband to a stop and locked his wheelchair in place. Looking at Sandra and Zayeda, then cutting an eye at Chavis before greeting Aaron with a smile.

"Hello. I'm Kaleico's Aunt." She gave him her hand. "Evelyn."

Chavis watched as Aaron took Evelyn's hand. Her husband next to her in his chair, head bobbing about, hands trembling as if they wanted to be raised but lacked the strength to do so.

Melvin began to grunt and drool aggressively.

Chantelle ran to her father's aid. "What's wrong daddy? You okay?" She knew there would be no reply, but that never stopped her from trying.

Everyone watched as she and Evelyn coddled him. Chavis stole a glance at Evelyn's ass as she squat in front of the chair and fumbled with the flaps. A view he always enjoyed. Especially when there was no clothing to cover it, and nothing to restrict the view of his manhood sliding inside.

She stood up, stealing a glance at Chavis over her shoulder. No one noticed, they were too busy watching her husband, feeling sorry for his state of being.

He'd been confined to the chair for years now. His function limited from the waist up, restricted completely from the waist down. Evelyn had spent a bulk of her life loving him in every way possible before the accident, but he never appreciated her. Even became abusive at times, now here he was, helpless.

No longer able to hurt her. She was able to smile now. Able to live. Not even her sister knew of Melvin's abusive past. He'd always been a saint in their eyes. If she were to speak of it now - now that he was hurt - no one would believe her. They'd all judge her, say that she left him just because he was an invalid.

An image she wasn't willing to don, especially in the eyes of her daughter. So she stayed. She stayed and she continued to care for him, just as her vows had promised. But she wasn't perfect.

No one knew this better than Chavis. His evidence the pool of tears that lay on his chest after their first sexual encounter. But after the first time she returned. Coming again and again.

Each time becoming less reserved. More willing. More wiley.

Chavis had slain her in every room of his home, in every position possible, but their time had run it's course. She'd become aggravating.

Evelyn kept up appearances. All smiles and giggles, talking to everyone in the room while fuming on the inside. She'd wanted to be with her secret lover last night but as Chavis often did, he'd rejected her. Declined her attempts to come visit.

Forced to stay home with nothing to do but watch her husband lay helpless in bed. Till desperation called and she found herself using his slobbering mouth for satisfaction. Mounting his face, bucking and rolling herself to pleasure, more so from the notion of humiliating the man who once terrorized her, knowing there wasn't a damn thing he could do about it.

Chavis grew tired of her evil eyeing. He rose from the table. "Thanks for the pancakes, Sandra." He kissed Kaleico's mother on the cheek.

"Where you running off to?" Sandra asked.

"I just got a few things I gotta take care of. I'll be back through to see yall later on."

He gave Kaleico a hug then held his fist out towards Aaron. Aaron's fist met his with a bump.

"Nice to meet you, dog." Chavis reaffirmed "We still on tonight, right?"

Aaron looked to Kaleico hoping she'd protest. She didn't. "It's cool." She shrugged. "It'll give us a chance to do some girl stuff."

Chavis slapped him on the shoulder. "It's settled then. See you this evening."

He gave Zayeda a playful nudge on the way out as he headed for the door.

"Bye Chavis!" The women chimed.

All except Evelyn.

Chapter 9

The air outside was brisk, biting at Kaleico's ankles as she took to the pavement. The balls of her feet striking at a rhythmic pace. Her running pants snug and warm as she moved along with Aaron at her heels.

She took her eyes off the road long enough to look over at him as he caught up. His arms pumping with each stride, biceps flexing through his tight fitted thermal top, she could only wonder where his mind was at the moment.

Aaron wasn't much the chatty type when exercising. She often teased he didn't have the wind for it. But he claimed he just preferred to listen to music, and enjoy the bliss that comes with running.

Rubbish. He just didn't have the endurance necessary to run and talk at the same time. Looking down at the bulge in his sweats, flopping around she reconsidered, then again he'd never had any real issues when it came to endurance, where it mattered most, in the bedroom.

She smiled. Looking over Aaron continued to speed along as he pulled the earbud from his ear and asked. "What you smiling for?"

"Nothing." She looked forward and sped up. "Keep up or get lost, slow poke!"

She took off forcing him to follow, cutting through side streets, running between houses, even jumping a few fences along the way, having to flee a barking dog or two before finding themselves backtracking towards her mother's house. This time approaching from the parallel street, one block over.

They came up on a split level that was a shadow of its past self. Aaron admired the house, despite the fact the paint was weathered and the lawn in need of tending it was nice.

He noticed someone in the doorway. He saw Kaleico in his peripheral waving to the person. It was Chavis. At that moment as they passed Aaron could see the back of Kaleico's mother's home, realizing for the first time their back yards were connected.

Kaleico called to Aaron "Don't conk out on me!" She looked back. "Come on. We're almost there." She teased.

He'd inadvertently slowed down. Snapping out of his trance he pepped his step and caught up with her. Rounding the block they sat foot on the street that connected the parallel roads. Turning on her mother's street they finished with an explosive sprint that ended in her mother's front drive.

"Whoo!" Kaleico celebrated.

Giving Aaron a high-five then a peck on the lips before bending over in front of him to stretch her hamstrings.

Holding her toes she looked back. "See something you like?"

Before he could reply the front door opened. Her sister leaned against the door frame, folding her arms over her chest.

She looked to Aaron. "Chavis said he'd be around to pick you up in a bit." Then to Kaleico. "And momma said we can go do some last minute shopping as soon as you got back." She looked at her watch. "So, if you don't mind."

Kaleico straightened up. Giving Aaron one last peck. "This is her way of telling me to hurry." Walking towards the house, talking over her shoulder. "You should hurry, too. Chavis will be here in a moment."

Aaron mumbled. "Didn't know I was into play dates." He resigned "But whatever."

Chapter 10

The crowded parking lot was filled with holiday shoppers. Aaron looked at the people coming and going like ants to an anthill, some leaving with gift filled bags where others such as themselves were just finding a spot to park.

"So this is our destination?" He asked Chavis.

"This would be it!" Chavis took the key from the ignition. "It's Christmas. I figured you'ld wanna do a little last minute shopping." He smirked. "That's what men do, right? Wait to the last minute?"

He stepped from the car, speaking over the roof as Aaron stepped out on the other side.

"Or, let me guess, Mr. Euber boyfriend already shopped!"

"Wh ...Nah. Nah I haven't sho ..." He changed the subject. "Didn't they say they were going to the mall too? Want we just run into them, kind of spoils the whole surprise thing.."

"Nah. Different mall. They'll do Concord. You know women like outlet type malls. Holiday deals and such."

He shut the car door and began to walk towards the entrance. Aaron followed.

Chavis added as an afterthought. "However. I'm sure once they're done getting their gifts, they'll probably come here later. You know how Kaleico is about shoes. She loves a deal, but when it comes to shoes, that girl holds no purse strings."

"Yeah.." Aaron replied. "You noticed too, huh?"

"I notice everything."

Aaron thought to himself. "Yeah. I noticed."

. . . . .

"Kaleico if you look at that phone one more time!" Sandra warned.

They'd enjoyed a day of shopping and were held up at a local restaurant, waiting for their appetizers to come.

"And you!" Sandra looked to Kaleico's sister. "How about you stop taking pictures and Instagramming everything around you, long enough to see what's in front of you." She shook her head. "So busy sharing your experience with the world, you ain't experienced it yourself."

Zayeda replied by snapping a photo of a drink, a long island, on someone else's table then texted the caption – mom won't let me order one of these #buzzkill. She read the caption aloud as she typed it.

"Hashtag, daughter thinks I want still whoop that ass!" Sandra snatched the phone and put it in her purse.

This made Kaleico laugh, until Sandra gestured for her phone with a few quick snaps of the fingers.

"Ma?"

"Come wit it! That man of yours is grown. He'll be okay. Chavis'll take care of him." She snapped again. "Come on. It's girl time. Hand it over!"

She did as asked but not before sending Aaron a quick text.

Lov you hope u enjoy yourself

Chapter 11

Aaron sat uncomfortably in the mall food court. He and Chavis were at a table surrounded by a flock of women whom Chavis had invited to join them.

One of the girls had volunteered herself to Aaron's phone which lay on the table and enjoyed a game of Candy Crush. He'd fought the urge to snatch it from her when she'd initially reached for it, but what was the harm. Eventually they'd finish chatting and giggling with Chavis, she'd put the phone down and they'd go along their merry way.

"Look." The girl leaned into Aaron showing him the screen. "High score!"

Thirty minutes and a high score later and his hopes of a quick departure had long gone down the drain.

Chavis on the opposite end of the table took notice of Aaron's discomfort. Reaching across the table he tapped the girl's busy hands.

"Alright. Enough Candy Crush. You're killing this poor guy's battery."

Chavis pried the phone from her grip, doing what Aaron had wanted to do all along.

The girl looked at Aaron as Chavis fumbled with the phone. She apologized as she leaned over and gave him a peck. "I'm sorry."

Aaron flinched. Chavis laughed as he continued to poke away at the phone. "Watch it now. That man got a woman at home." He pressed anther button and looked up at Aaron. "Checking my Facebook. You don't mind, do you?"

"Nah." Aaron replied.

Chavis returned the phone to the screen saver then handed it to him. Relieved to have his device back in his grips Aaron smiled. A smile that quickly faded when the phone's battery beacon displayed 'low' then deactivated itself.

"Damn."

Chavis looked at his watch. "Alright ladies. It's been a privilege meeting you all but me and my friend here have some places to be." He looked around. "Besides. The malls closing, they're not gonna let us spend the night."

He eyed one of the girls.

"However. If they did, I'd imagine we'd find ourselves napping somewhere in the middle of Victoria's Secret."

They all laughed and said their goodbye's, but not without Chavis making arrangements to hook up on a later date sometime in the near future.

Chavis waved goodbye then faced Aaron. "Now. Let's get up outta here. Its due time we get to the good stuff." Slapping him on the back. "Let me show you what this city's all about!"

CHAPTER 12

The club setting wasn't Aaron's usual scene. Uncomfortable as the stiff backed seats were, he'd never imagined they'd be made less comfortable by a woman's presence.

Chavis sat next to him laughing himself to tears. A half-naked woman straddling him, gyrating he stuffed a few bills then handed a few to Aaron who also had a topless woman in front of him, ass first, looking back at him through her legs while her head and palms grazed the floor, both cheeks clapping in unison on beat to the music.

The closer her ass got the further he drew back, pressing so hard against the back of the chair the front legs began to raise up off the floor. Reaching over Chavis grabbed the back of the seat to prevent him from tipping over.

Chavis chuckled. "Come on, dog. What you scared of? It's just ass!"

Aaron's seat rocked forward the forelegs finding the floor, lurching him towards the ass wobbling in front of him. So close he could identify the fragrance used to flower her taint.

She raised up, slapping herself on the ass and asked. "You like that?"

"Umm …" He stuttered.

"He loooves it!" Chavis threw money at her then showered the girl on his own lap with more ones.

This made Aaron's companion become more aggressive, plopping down on his lap wriggling him to a lump in his briefs.

"Oooh." She cooed. "He does like it!" She giggled. "Alot!"

"My Man!" Chavis praised throwing more money. "Now you growing a pair! Now you growing a pair!"

Aaron didn't care much for Chavis' random here and there remarks. He wasn't ashamed in the least about the fact he was mad about Kaleico. Whenever he was around her she was all he could see, and when he was away from her, all he could envision. Even now, with another woman on his lap, all he wanted to do was get back to her.

He hadn't heard from her all day. The Candy Crush girl at the mall had killed his phone. He'd almost asked Chavis to use his till he'd teased "Looks like you won't be able to check in with mommy now."

He'd guaranteed Chavis that would be no issue. He would be fine. Kaleico knew he was out with him. If she wanted to contact him and couldn't reach him by his phone, she could call Chavis. If not, then she'd just have to wait till they returned.

However he never expected they'd be out this long, nor did he count on her going this long without attempting to at least contact Chavis and inquire about their whereabouts. Maybe she was just enjoying her time with her family? Or maybe she was enjoying time away from him.

Fine. If his absence didn't effect her any. Why should hers effect him any at all? The voice of Tequila reasoned. A drink he'd never had till tonight. A drink Chavis insisted he would enjoy all the more if he made sure to eat the worm, when taking his fourth shot.

Maybe it was the Tequila, or the ass in his lap, or maybe the notion Kaleico obviously wasn't missing him at the moment that made him relax? Whatever the case he suddenly found comfort in the shifting and shimmying of the semi-nude girl who now whirled around, lifting a leg over his chest, using her tongue to trace his neck.

Aaron's eyes rolled into his head. Vision obstructed by his eyelids he couldn't see Chavis sitting next to him, staring intently.

Ignoring the girl rolling on his own lap Chavis just watched him, wondering what made him so special? Why would Kaleico bring home someone like this? Pushing the girl off his lap he stood and fished his phone from his pocket. Kaleico had called, looking for her boyfriend no doubt. The same boyfriend that sat in front of him right now. Another woman on his lap. Ass cupped in his hands, eyes closed in a heat of passion. Not thinking about Kaleico at all.

Chavis was sure, at the moment, Aaron wasn't thinking about anything ..... Other than himself.

Pointing his phone Chavis pressed a button, scrolling through the options, he made a few more taps at the screen as he turned and headed for the bar to get himself, and an already incoherent Aaron, yet another drink.

Chapter 13

Zayeda lay in bed watching an episode of Dead End Road on her I-pad when a muffled series of rants worked their way to her ear, via the vent on her floorboard.

Pressing pause she removed her earbuds and crawled from the bed, creeping towards the vent as if someone could see her eaves dropping on the makeshift com.

It was Kaleico, downstairs in Zayeda's old room fussing at Aaron. Zayeda knew that her sister wasn't supposed to be in there with him partaking in any monkey business, their mother would kill he and Kaleico both, but it appeared sex wasn't on the menu.

Zayeda looked at her watch it was the early a.m. hours. Apparently Kaleico had stayed up, waiting by the front door, just to give Aaron the business for staying out so late.

One thing for certain, Zayeda jumped up grabbing a candy bar from her drawer before laying down by the vent, propping herself on an elbow as she enjoyed a snack, she wasn't about to miss any of this.

.....

"Shhhush!" Aaron hushed. "Kaleico you're gonna make your momma .... You're not even supposed to be in here with ... she's gonna think we're down here.."

A slap to the noggin stopped his tongue mid-sentence.

"Don't you worry about my momma right now!" Kaleico's tone low and aggressive. "You better worry about the fact her wrath is mine, by way of genetics!" She snatched a pillow from the bed and knocked him towards the dresser with it.

"Agghh! Girl stop!" He held an arm over his face as she continued to fling it with all her might.

Perfume bottles toppled and rattled on the dresser's surface when he bumped into it. Catching an opening he grabbed her elbows, shaking the pillow from her grips. Taking it from her, it now played shield from the flailing palms that came his way.

"Coming in this house in the a.m. like you crazy!" She fussed. "Embarrassing me in front of my ..."

"Aye." He dropped the pillow and trapped her wrist, pushing her towards the bed till she fell onto it. "You the one who wanted me to play buddy with your lil'" He said in a mocking tone. "Childhood friend ... like a brother to me ... Friend of the family."

He glared down at her, eyes alcohol glazed and serious. She felt him pressing her tight against the mattress. Looking up at him she suddenly found herself ceasing to resist.

"Aaron?" She cocked her head. "Wait a minute.." She reached cradling his face. "You're not jealous are you?"

"Jealou ..." He snickered. "Yeah right. Of what? That guy?"

She let her hands slide down his chest and around his waist. "Cause if you are.." her hand found his buckle. "I just want you to know.." She unfastened it. "You got nothing," She put her hand down the front of his briefs. "Absolutely nothing at all" Pulling his manhood from its pouch. "To worry about."

. . ....

Zayeda lay by the vent. Rolling her eyes she decided a few grunts and moans were more than she could bare. Crawling to her feet she threw the candy bar wrapper in the trash can and plopped back onto her bed.

"Men are too easy." She thought in a low whisper.

Grabbing her I-pad she switched from the show she'd paused to another screen. A series of photographs. Rubbing her fingers over the pictures she selected one, enlarging it.

But to some women the hearts of certain men seemed to come especially easy.

She examined the man on the screen.

These were the type of woman, whom women like herself despised.

She gave the picture one last glance tossing it aside. The screen slowly faded to black, taking with it the image of Chavis, standing in a window half dressed, with a towel on his waist.

Chapter 14

The receding hum of an engine made Aaron stir to a flicker of consciousness. Opening one eye just a wink he pulled the worn blanket over his head and nestled his face in the pillow.

The sound of approaching footsteps and light chatter caused him to open both eyes. The voice outside the bedroom door got closer. "I'll get him."

A rap at the door made him raise up. Tossing the covers aside he realized he was naked. The door creaked open.

"Aaron." It was Zayeda, Kaleico's sister. "Oh!"

Aaron rolled to grab the covers from the floor. Realizing this exposed his ass he opted to just roll all the way to the floor. Landing atop of the blanket, wrapping himself in it.

Zayeda giggled. He blushed. She didn't. There was no sign of embarrassment evident on her part.

"Breakfast is ready." She stood, watching, waiting.

"Oh." He pulled the covers over his exposed chest as he stood. "Alright ... I ... I'll be right out."

She smiled, leaning on the doorframe for an awkward moment. Kaleico's voice came from the kitchen.

"Is he up?"

"Yeah." Zayeda yelled over her shoulder, then looked towards Aaron's covered pelvis. "He up." She grabbed the doorknob and pulled the door closed, exiting with one final downward glance. "Way to go, buddy!"

Aaron followed her gaze. The door closed as she left him to stare at the early morning hard-on in question.

Throwing the blanket aside he spoke to his rigid flesh. "Well, introduce yourself to everybody while you're at it!"

Shaking his head he rustled his boxers from the floor and prepped himself to join the rest for breakfast.

·····

"Well, there he is!" Kaleico chimed as Aaron entered.

A look around and he quickly noted they were once again entertaining early morning company. It was Melvin, Kaleico's Uncle. He'd been introduced to the wheelchair bound man and his wife just yesterday. She wasn't around today, but her daughter, Kaleico's cousin Chantelle was.

Sitting next to her father Chantelle smiled as Kaleico jumped from the table and met her man with a morning kiss.

"Spruuung!" Chantelle teased before spooning a bit of oatmeal into her father's mouth.

Zayeda sat across from her. Sandra behind her reaching over her, pouring more juice into her glass as she spiked a pile of pancakes from the plate, stuffing them in her mouth, detesting Kaleico's constant cry for attention.

"Good morning!" Sandra greeted him. "Kaleico let that boy go! Over there smothering him. Let him sit down and eat!" She gestured towards an empty seat with a full plate awaiting.

He took a seat, doing his best not to look overly-sympathetic for the drooling man adjacent to him. Chantelle spooned another lump of oatmeal to her father. Ogling over him as she wiped at the corner of his mouth.

"So, Aaron." Chantelle faced him. "Enjoying our quaint little city so far?"

"Yeah." He nodded taking a bite of pancakes. "I gotta say, Charlotte's not so bad."

Chantelle held a cup, with a straw to her father's lips. Aaron tried to focus on her-not the clear straw, struggling to pull juice to his mouth as she replied. "Not such a bad place to think about packing up and moving to, huh?"

"Girl." Kaleico cut in. "Leave my man alone. Ain't nobody moving nowhere. You just want me down here so you can get on my nerves every day."

The two shared a laugh. Sandra finally took a seat, treating herself to a bite. "Aaron, don't pay those two no mind." She pursed her lips and blew on her coffee before sipping.

Her lips were like Kaleico's, gorgeous. In fact as Aaron looked around the table he noticed those lips seemed to extend throughout the family. They all had an eerie resemblance from the mother, all the way down to the cousin.

Zayeda cleared her throat, looking at Aaron. "I heard you had somewhat of a good time, last night."

Aaron assumed she was referring to his staying out late. She wasn't.

Kaleico knowing her sister all too well thought about the vent. She glared at her daring

74

her to let on that she'd heard Kaleico in the room with Aaron, last night.

Sandra addressed it. "Stay out of people's business." She assumed, like Aaron she meant his staying out late. "Besides, Kaleico knew he was out with Chavis last night." She reached over and clasped Aaron's fist. "He was in good hands."

Patting him on the shoulder she turned her attention back to the plate in front of her.

Chantelle affirmed "Yeah. Chavis definitely gonna make sure you come home, safe and sound."

Her father began to grunt when Kaleico, remembering something began to laugh.

She asked "Hey, do you remember that time you were at that party and you had to call Chavis to come get you, because that guy …"

"Umm okay!" Chantelle leaned over and covered her father's ears. "My daddy is, right here. It was supposed to be a secret, remember?"

Sandra chided "Chavis been here for us all, at one point or another." Pointing around the table. "Every single one of us."

Chantelle's father grunted more, this time drooling intensely.

"Awe." She talked to him like a baby. "He's getting aggravated." Wiping his mouth again. "Don't worry daddy. Ma will be back soon." She looked at her watch. "She better be anyway! I got an appointment to get to."

She produced her phone dialing her mother's number, receiving no answer she followed with a text. Frustration apparent on her face she sat the phone on the table and checked her watch again.

Sandra asked. "Where you gotta be?"

"Nowhere special." She shrugged. "I just was suppose to check up on this job offer but.."

"Unh!" Sandra jumped from her seat. "Did this girl say job?" She ran to the wall and grabbed her keys. "I know she ain't say, Job!" She walked over and dangled the keys in her face. "Here. Get where you got to go, honey and get there before it snow! Cause if you talking bout working somewhere, it's sure finna be some snowflakes falling!"

She began to sing White Christmas. Chantelle didn't like being the butt of anyone's joke but she took the keys and looked to her father.

"Don't worry." Sandra assured her. "We got him." Pushing Chantelle towards the door. "I'm sure your momma will be back soon. Besides Melvin can't fit in that car anyway, with the chair and all."

Zayeda jumped from her seat. "Shotgun!" Not wanting to spend any more time in the house than necessary.

Kaleico knew that her sister's hasty reaction was intended to one-up her for the front seat. Chantelle looked to see if she was joining them.

"Yall go ahead." Kaleico waved. "I'm gonna stay here and help mom around the house."

"Suit yourself!" Chantelle made for the door with Zayeda trailing behind.

Kaleico took a napkin from the table and attempted to wipe at Melvin's mouth. He grunted and drooled even more.

Sandra nudged her aside. "It's alright, sweety" she began to clean him up. "Your daughter will be back soon and your wife before that."

He calmed. Kaleico took a seat at the far end of the table, waiting for a moment she rose. "I'm about to go shower!"

Aaron called to her as she walked away. "Not running today?"

"No I was up late, remember? I'll take a rain check."

"Have it your way." He looked to see that Sandra was cleaning the table. "I'm about to help your mom do the dishes, just in case you need time to change your mind."

He joined Sandra at the sink. She tried to decline but he insisted. Grabbing the scrub brush, pointing to the towel. He'd wash, she'd dry and Kaleico's Uncle could sit there and watch.

. . . . .

"Oh God! Chavis!" Evelyn's nails burrowed down in his chest

His shoulders pressed hard into the mattress, hips bridged upward the balls of his feet held him steady while his cock played hold for her straddled thighs and open vulva. Punctuating his presence with an occasional downward tug on her waist. Making her writhe in pain.

"Chavis! Mnnmm … Chavis! Mnmmmn oh God!"

She had begged to be hurt, to be punished. Texting him. Showing up at his door in the a.m. Her husband just one block away, a backyard between them, left to be watched over like a child or a pet, while she went searching for pleasure.

Pleasure that came in the form of pain and a sense of helplessness.

"I'm coming. I'm com.. I'm coming!" Her voice filled the room.

She found release and with that came relief. But, as she knew it would, it came with a price.

Having allowed her a sense of joy, a moment of ecstasy. Chavis rolled her over till she was trapped beneath him, flipping her onto her stomach without retracting himself he took her from behind.

"Wait ... Chavis. Wait baby... Just let me rest a second. Just let me... Please just let me..Mnnagghh! Agghhh! Mnnn! Mnnnnaghh aghh aghh!"

.....

Aaron looked at Kaleico's mother as they stood by the sink. "Mrs. Thompson"

"Sandra! She insisted.

"Umn..Sandra." He handed her a plate after rinsing it. "I just wanna say, I'm sorry if I said anything wrong yesterday. Concerning your husband's passing."

"Humph." She took the plate and toweled it dry. "Passin." She put the plate in the rack, looking at the ceiling then Aaron. "I'm not sure that's what they call it, when you take your own life, sweety."

Aaron froze. Mouth open without words, lost.

Sandra looked. "Wait ... How exactly did you think my husband died?"

"Un..I..Kaleico never, she just said he got sick and"

"Sick." She said the word doubtfully. "Kaleico loved her father. I suppose its only right she made up excuses for what he did."

"What did he.."

She cut him off. "Hung his self, right back there, in the backyard." She walked back over to give Melvin's mouth a wipe then continued. "Hung himself on the privacy fence, right by the pool."

Aaron was confused "Pool?"

She took a seat. "It's gone now." Waving her hand. "Just made me think about him too much. We filled it in, long time ago. Only thing left was the fence and Chavis did me the service of tearing that down, not very long ago."

Aaron stood by the sink watching as she drift into thought then continued.

"Good thing he did. Seeing that old fence would've just been a constant reminder for Kaleico of the day she …. Found him." Her eyes teared up. "Just hanging there. Dead. Forever."

He walked over to give her a hug as she began to sob.

"Bastard just killed himself and nobody know why. No note. No warning. Nothing. Nothing at all."

81

She gently pushed Aaron away and composed herself. Clearing her throat, wiping her eyes she showed the same resilience he'd seen displayed numerous times by the very child she birthed.

"That had to have been traumatic." He thought out loud. "For Kaleico I mean. Finding him like that."

Sandra nodded. "Looked out her bedroom window and there he was." She sat down. "Poor things first instinct was to run straight out the door, to try to get him down." She remembered. "By the time I woke from the sounds of her screams and ran out the door to see what was wrong, Chavis had already come running to her aid. I walked outside just as he'd climbed the fence and cut the rope. Just in time to see my dead husband fall to the ground in a heap. Right into my crying child's open arms."

She shook her head.

"I think that day brought her and Chavis together, closer than ever. I was no good to anyone for a while, I fell apart, Chavis was there to give her comfort during a time when I couldn't even comfort myself. He helped her when I couldn't." She wiped her eyes.

Melvin began to grunt and squirm in his chair.

Sandra continued. "For that, I'll always love that boy." She added then grabbed a towel to wipe at his mouth. "Then when Kaleico got old enough to go off to college. I guess you can say he went from comforting her to catering to me."

Melvin kept squirming, Aaron listened.

"Cutting the grass, carrying groceries. Any and everything I could ever want or need, Chavis is there." She smiled. "And I guess it was only right, when his mother passed a few years back, I took to catering to him a bit. Guess you could say, we all keep an eye on each other. Like family supposed to."

This time she smiled and this made Aaron smile in reply.

.....

Kaleico stood in her old bedroom. Hair wet from the shower, she searched for her sister's blow dryer. She noticed there was none of the usual décor normal for a teenage girl. The main thing being a heart shaped frame, with some boys face in it, on the dresser.

"Hmmmnn." Kaleico wondered." Maybe she's gay?" She drew an inquiring hashtag in the air then uttered. "Seems to be trending."

Unable to find the blow dryer she wrapped the towel around her head and took a bottle of perfume from the dresser. Giving herself a spritz as she turned and caught a glimpse of something out the window.

Looking across the backyard she could see a silhouette in Chavis' window. A woman. Breast flopping about as she moved about the room, then she saw a naked Chavis come to the window.

"Babe!" Aaron's voice called up the stairs, making her jump.

She looked towards the door. "Up here! I'm in my roo.. In Zayeda's room." She reminded herself.

Running up the stairs Aaron peeped into the room, seeing that she was in a bathrobe, with her hair dripping wet under the towel on her head.

Upon observation he stated. "A definite no, on the run then?"

"Definite!" She grabbed his hand and pulled him into the room.

He whispered. "What are you..Your mom's right downstairs."

She dropped the towel exposing herself. Raising a brow he looked behind him then pulled the door shut. Kaleico tugged him against her, breast touching his chest as she kissed him then turned herself so that her backside pressed against the bulge in his sweats.

Her back to him she now faced the window again. Noting very quickly the window at the opposite end of the backyard-Chavis' window was now closed, the curtains drawn tight.

Aaron began to kiss her on the neck, cupping her breast from behind.

She bumped him with her rear, knocking him back. "Stop boy." She turned and slapped his arm. "You know my momma down there."

"Oh. So you just gonna tease me like that?"

She gave him a kiss on the cheek then bent to grab her robe from the floor. Pointing to his erection. "How about you go run that off!"

She blew him a kiss then made an exit.

"Won't be the first time I ran a Three-legged race!" He shot back in reply.

Chapter 15

The frigid air formed light burst of smoke in wake of every exhaled breath expelled from Aaron's lungs as he began a slow trot, allowing his legs time to warm up before taking a steady, much faster pace.

Today he'd run the same route except in reverse. Rounding the corner he soon found himself in view of Chavis' front drive. In it a green family van with a large handicap sign on its rear bumper with another sticker that read Wheelchair Accessible.

Getting closer to the mailbox he saw the front door open in his peripheral. A woman appeared then quickly moved away from the door, just as he'd caught a glimpse of her, grooming her hair and adjusting the bra behind her partially buttoned blouse.

Before he could see her face clearly she was nudged aside by Chavis who stood with a towel around his waist, waving hello to Aaron as he passed.

Stepping out barefoot Chavis shouted. "Still got gas in the tank, I see!"

Aaron's headphones drowned his words. Not sure what he'd said Aaron just gave him a thumbs up and kept going. Increasing speed in fact. He didn't know what he said, nor did he care. There was just something about him that didn't sit right with Aaron. No matter how much Kaleico and her family loved him. Aaron dared to think that he, personally, did not like him at all.

Keeping straight till he found the next corner he made another turn, doing his best to remember the entire route taken the day before. Hoping his decision to run it in the opposite direction would do nothing to throw him off. He'd left his phone at the house. He definitely didn't want to end up lost.

·····

Forty minutes had passed and he'd found himself just a minute away from Kaleico's mother's home. It wasn't his best time but considering he'd been on an all-night binge there was no shame in a little decline in time.

Seeing the street he sought he made a sharp left, his pace shifting to low gear as he set eyes on something that threw him off. The green van. Looking around he checked his bearings, making sure he hadn't somehow made his way back to Chavis' street. It wasn't, he was on the right road. It was the right house, Sandra's house, only the vehicle parked in front of it had changed locations.

Coincidence maybe? There were thousands of green vans he thought. Then he came to a screeching halt, bringing his run to a close, stopping right in front of the driveway.

Catching his breath, he looked at the bumper.

A handicap sign. Wheelchair Accessible.

.....

Sandra opened the door, smile forever plastered welcoming Aaron back from his run. "Look at you all sweaty and ship shape-like!"

He laughed. A glance over her shoulder and he saw Kaleico's Aunt Evelyn, hovering over her husband fumbling with his shirt collar. Aaron noticed her own blouse seemed to be in better order than when he'd seen her at the beginning of his run.

He hadn't recognized her then, in Chavis' doorway but the van out front, alongside her familiar attire was all the confirmation he needed. No doubt she was the half clothed woman in question.

Evelyn looked up meeting his eyes, quickly dropping her gaze to the floor. The look on her face like a cat next to an empty birdcage with a canary in its mouth.

Aaron thought. "Now look at her hanging all over her husband like she just returned from the market. Then again maybe it was normal for Kaleico's Aunt to hang around half naked men. Especially Chavis." Aaron scoffed. "He is like family."

Kaleico came down the stairs, as Sandra stepped aside so Aaron could enter.

Aaron met her as she approached. "Hey babe."

"Unuh." She stiff armed. "No hug for you, dirty boy." Side stepping slapping him on the rear. "Not till after you wash that funk away!"

"Dammit" Evelyn cursed causing them all to look.

She was having difficulty dealing with Melvin's chair. She quickly went into a distressful rant that ended in a light sob.

Sandra ran to her sister's aid. "Oh Sweety." Helping her with the chair. "It's nothing, just jammed a bit."

After a moment Sandra realized her luck was no better.

"Aaron." She asked "Honey could you …"

"Yeah." Aaron wiped his sweaty palms on his shirt. "Sure I can help."

He walked over and with a few tugs the problem was solved.

"Thank you." Evelyn kept her head down as she thanked him.

Sandra added. "Thank you. That always gets stuck. Good thing you're here. Chavis usually ..."

Melvin began to grunt angrily. Grabbing Aaron's wrist with his limp hand. Aaron tensed.

"Wha..." Aaron looked around. "What is he trying to say?"

Evelyn stepped in, grabbing the chair pulling him away from Aaron. "He probably just has to relieve himself. Or has relieved himself rather." She corrected. "I'm just gonna take him to the bathroom." She pulled an Adult diaper from her bag and pushed him out of the room.

Sandra gave Aaron a reassuring pat. "Thanks Sweety."

Kaleico came over and kissed his temple. "Aunt Evelyn can take it from here. Go ahead and get your shower out the way, she got it."

Aaron nodded taking a few steps he thought of something. "You know there's an interesting, inexpensive App I once saw in a Tech magazine. All you need is an I-pad. It recognizes ocular movement and he can use the program to type what he's thinking, or say what he ..."

Kaleico pinched his cheeks and kissed him on the lips this time. "Shower!" She reiterated then, reminded. "They've been dealing with Uncle Melvin a long time. They've got it."

The front door opened. It was Kaleico's sister and cousin.

Chantelle entered with a frown as Evelyn reappeared. "Ma! Where were you? You know I had that job thing."

This was Aaron's cue to leave but not without one last utterance. "I still say he'd like to have a say." He spoke of her Uncle before jetting up the stairs.

Kaleico called after him. "Oh yeah, I almost forgot. I need you to hurry up. We got somewhere to be in an hour." She added. "A family outing!"

Chapter 16

The most shocking part of Aaron's day would have been if the 'family outing' hadn't included Chavis. But of course he was there. Surprise.

Chavis had met up with them earlier in the day at a local church, their first stop. Aaron had watched the entire time as Kaleico's Aunt and Chavis made sure to play on opposite ends of the room almost everywhere they ended up.

The evasive maneuvers seemed to be more so on Evelyn's part. Either Chavis didn't know that Aaron alleged of illicit activity between the two or he didn't care, his demeanor showed signs of the latter. Evelyn on the other hand seemed not so comfortable with the thought of anyone even being suspicious of the fact.

Aaron and Kaleico had taken the backseat, Sandra driving as she and Zayeda, riding up front with her, argued over the radio stations all the way from their home to the church. Behind them Evelyn trailed with Chantelle and her husband alongside her in the van.

Once they'd arrived Aaron shook a few hands and exchanged a smile or two with a few people introduced to him by Sandra, others by Kaleico, even Chavis introduced him to a few.

"Kaleico's latest and newest catch." He'd called him, with a hearty laugh and slap on the shoulder.

What an asshole.

There had been no early morning service. They'd only stopped by the church to gather a few supplies. Joining many others who'd brought along contributions of canned foods and other essentials, all of which were loaded onto a truck and hauled to a nearby shelter, where everyone including the Pastor tagged along to provide a nice warm meal to the homeless. "An early Merry Christmas."

Even the half-starved seemed willing to trade their chance at a meal for a moment to ogle over Chavis. But no attention spent in his honor was more annoying than that of Kaleico. Maybe she believed in the whole 'like family' thing, but now that Aaron suspected he was screwing Aunt Evelyn, he felt there was room to suspect he'd do the same to her.

Then again wouldn't any man?

The soup kitchen. The ride back to the church in which, against Aaron's better judgment, Kaleico decided they'd ride with Chavis. Even the time spent at the church, winding down from a day of good service seemed to be filled with everyone, including the Preacher's wife, spending the bulk of their time saying, 'Chavis. Chavis. Chavis.'

Chavis this. Chavis that. Aaron was sick of it. He was glad to see the day end. Of course that wasn't until after the Pastor begged Chavis to play the organ and sing a rendition of Silent Night before allowing everyone to part ways.

"How bout we go hang out a while?" Chavis suggested as they walked across the church parking lot.

Aaron made it a point to head for Sandra's car, already reaching for the rear passenger door, when Kaleico decided for the both of them.

"Why not?" She told Chavis. "I could use a little fun!"

Chavis extended "Sandra?"

"No. No. No" Sandra giggled. "I'm gonna leave the young people stuff to yall. I'm calling it a night."

"I'm going!" Zayeda volunteered.

Sandra snapped. "Oh, no you don't!"

"But Ma!" She plead. "You just said they were going to do young people stuff."

Sandra confirmed. "21 and older, type young stuff. Not almost 18, and in a hurry to be 21 type stuff."

"But." She whined. "My birthday only so far away."

Sandra rolled her eyes and faced Aaron. "She think turning 18 mean, the world will be hers to do what she want with." She looked at Zayeda. "Get your butt in this car, now. Or don't make it to see another birthday."

Embarrassed, Zayeda lowered her head and disappeared into the passenger seat. Aaron wished he could do the same but the fact Kaleico now stood by Chavis' car waiting indicated the contrary.

Chantelle, Kaleico's cousin gave her dad a kiss on the cheek, handing the charge of the wheelchair to her mother she told her. "I'm going with them!"

She wasted no time claiming shotgun as Chavis climbed behind the wheel, and Aaron reluctantly joined in the backseat.

Chapter 17

The bar was cluttered. People rambled about in gaudy unattractive sweaters and hats. It appeared they'd walked unexpectedly into an 'ugly Christmas sweater party.'

Kaleico nudged Aaron pointing out a bright lit man donning a sweater covered in Christmas lights. He walked by them raising his glass, nodding at them as he passed. "Merry Christmas!"

"Merry Christmas." Kaleico chimed.

Aaron loved to see her smile. Why was he moping, worrying about some family friend stepping on his toes? This guy was nobody. No comparison. Aaron knew when it came down to it he was the apple of her eye.

Wrapping an arm around her he became a participant, pointing out a few sweaters of his own.

The rest of the night was spent sharing stories from the past. Kaleico's cousin, Chantelle brought up all Kaleico's most embarrassing secrets, half of which Chavis nod in agreement to, as if it were previously shared Intel.

The Christmas music blared non-stop, egg-nog and other spirits in constant flow. The tunes stopping only long enough for the D.J. to call up all the ugly sweater contestants to the front, where the patrons were allowed to choose a winner.

Christmas light man was runner up, with heavy praise found himself taking a plastic trophy, a silver Christmas tree. While the grand prize went to a female in a transparent long sleeve top, made of clear plastic. Double-lined and filled with liquid and tiny white flakes that float around and cascaded all over her plastic frame whenever she jumped herself into a shaken frenzy.

"And the winner is …. SANTA'S MISTRESS!"

The whistles and catcalls mingled with the applause and clanging of glass, till finally the music returned and the party commenced.

Chantelle started. "I think the winner should've been ….urgghh!"

Chavis jumped out of the way as she puked on the floor.

"Whoa!" Aaron moved, jumping behind Kaleico for cover.

Kaleico became momma hen at that moment. "Okay sweety. Somebody's had enough festivities for the night."

Coming to her aid Chavis grabbed a scarf, a monstrosity of a knit job given to him by one of his fan girls at the church. He'd draped it over his shoulders when she'd gifted him with it earlier, where it remained until they'd entered the bar and he'd tossed it over the back of the seat.

Kaleico saw that he was about to use the pea-green and purple plaid creation to wipe Chantelle's mouth when she stopped him.

"Unuh. I got it!" The scarf was ugly she agreed, but a gift nonetheless. No need to mess it up.

Using a napkin she began to clean Chantelle's chin as she flagged someone to let them know there was a mess on the floor.

Chavis stepped aside, stuffing the scarf in his back pocket so that it dangled to his calf, making room for a young waiter/busboy, looking a day under 21, to come heed their call. Upon arrival he realized he'd been flagged, not to proffer another round of drinks but to clean up a mess.

The disdain was clear and unmasked. "Ah. Man."

Kaleico apologized. "Sorry. She's just a little sick."

He mumbled. "You think?"

"Excuse me?" She frowned.

Aaron and Chavis both cocked their heads.

Still mumbling under his breath the busboy walked a bit too close to Kaleico as he passed, bumping her shoulder he mocked. "Sorry. She's just sick." He kept walking "Fuck this. I need a break."

"Hey!" Aaron took a step behind him.

"Aaron." Kaleico grabbed his arm. "Come on. Let's just go."

Chavis shook his head in disbelief. Taking Chantelle' arm, he watched the Waiter head towards one of the rear exits.

"Don't worry about that asshole." He ushered Chantelle towards the door with Kaleico and Aaron leading the way. "Let's get outta here."

Making it to the car they stuffed Chantelle in the front passenger seat. Chavis got behind the wheel with Aaron and Kaleico in the back.

The engine came to life and the heat began to blow out of the vents, helping to calm the shivers Kaleico had suddenly developed.

"Damn." Chavis looked around, fumbling through his pockets. "My phone!" He looked back. "Gimme one second. I left my phone on the table."

He jumped out and ran back to the bars entrance. Aaron looked at Kaleico as Chavis disappeared into the doorway.

Kaleico blushed "What?"

"You know what." Aaron smirked, leaning over nibbling on her ear. "What's up. You sneaking in my room tonight?"

She pulled his face to hers nibbling on his lip. "I don't know? It depends."

"Depends on what?"

"I'm really digging dudes in ugly sweaters tonight." She winked. "You got any ugly sweaters in your room."

He kissed her back. "Hmmm. I'm sure I can work out something."

.....

Chavis went through the front door. B-lining straight towards the emergency exit by the bars kitchen area. He'd seen the young boy head this way.

He pushed the door, the scent of smoke creeping through as it opened. The young boy stood by the dumpster, a cigarette in one hand and phone in the other.

Chavis felt his pocket vibrate as he stepped outside closing the door quietly. Good thing he had it on silent. It would've been hard to explain if it had rang just when he'd declared "I left my phone."

The busboy's back was turned as Chavis approached. Puffs of smoke rising above him while he spoke to someone on the phone. "Baby you gotta understand, I'm new to this being a dad thing. But I promise I'm gonna get outta this dump and get a real job then we'll get our own place. I promise, by the time the baby's one, we'll be out of my mom's house and we'll be one happy family. Okay? Alright. I love you. Bye."

The boy turned around. He thought he'd heard something but no one was there. He looked around to be sure. Nothing. He shrugged it off and walked towards the door, when a tug from behind pulled him off his feet.

"Aye .. What the ..." words lost in the pit of his gut.

Back slammed against the dumpster he couldn't breathe. The impact had dazed him. Vision blurred by watered eyes he saw Chavis come into focus. A huge fist barreling into the bridge of his nose made the young boy lose sight of him again.

He coiled over, only to have himself raised back up with a knee to the face. A ball of blood rolled from his lips, oozing towards the ground as he struggled to speak. "What I do?"

Chavis didn't reply instead he slammed him against the dumpster again, then punched him in the gut before tossing him to the ground.

"Please." The boy barely managed. "Please."

Chavis put a foot on his back, stopping him mid-crawl.

Reaching down he knelt before him.

"Please" The boys eyes were tear stained. "My … I have a daughter."

Chavis took his collar, dragging him on his belly to a cement platform that was raised just five-inches off the ground.

Palming the back of his head he slammed it to the concrete, knocking him unconscious. Then he placed his open mouth on the raised concrete edge, so that his upper row of teeth rest on its rim, while his lower jaw dangled off the end.

The boy was out cold, unaware of the menacing figure towering over him. Chavis stood tall, knee raised high, his foot hovering over the back of the boy's head. Till he brought it down with a devastating stomp. Cracking his top row of teeth. Shattering them on the concrete as his upper and lower jaw hinged two different ways.

·····

Aaron and Kaleico flinched at the sound of the car door opening. Their lips separating with a lusty resin of saliva dangling between them as Chavis hopped in.

"Did I disturb yall?" He looked back and laughed. Turning around he put the car in gear. "How bout I get yall kids home!"

"Did you find your phone?" Aaron asked as he pulled away.

"Yeah." He pat his pocket. "Right where I left it."

Chapter 18

Frustrated Zayeda sat in her room scanning the computer for any relevant messages or emails, smiling when she saw one that caught her eye.

Opening it the message read: Almost legal

She typed in reply: soon and very soon! #18

Anticipation stirring her hormones into a frenzy she couldn't wait. Didn't want to wait. If it were up to her she'd have long given herself to him, but he'd insisted, she had to wait. The closer she came to womanhood however and the more she'd come to know herself, she began to realize she didn't *have* to do anything at all.

She heard something through the vent, something rustling about, then the sound of a door creaking open downstairs. She knew that Kaleico and Aaron had returned some hours ago. Having stepped out of her room, peering down the stairs, she'd seen them lug a drunk Chantelle in the house and place her on the couch.

Aaron had attempted to pull Kaleico to his room but after a moment of teasing she wagged a finger and declined. Running up the stairs but not before Zayeda had managed to ease back into her room, closing the door without being spotted.

.....

Downstairs Aaron stepped from the room, walking the wrong way at first he quickly remembered he wasn't home and re-directed himself on the right path, leading towards the bathroom.

The hard liquor and natural urges had left him with a stiff erection that made it difficult to relieve his bladder. After a long awkward moment he managed a light trickle then finally a few hard jettisoned streams. Erection unwavering he ended with a shake and staggered out into the hall.

Going to the kitchen he fixed himself a glass of water to fend off dehydration, left behind by Tequila. Opening the fridge he stood there scratching himself for a moment then decided food wasn't on the menu. Leaving the kitchen, passing Chantelle, sprawled out on the couch he returned to the bedroom and closed the door behind him.

Falling to the bed he quickly found himself returning to a state of slumber. Dreamland welcomed him in the form of a soft, marshmallowy cloud that rest beneath his prone body. Holding him afloat the cloud carried him through the air. The light breeze tickling his ear made him smile. Rolling onto his side the fluffy cloud formed perfectly to his frame, contoured to provide maximum comfort as he drift along through the sky in a peaceful serene world of bliss.

Another breeze traipsed across his ear. This time the wind carried with it traces of rain. Not a hard torrential rain but a gentle dew that danced softly on the side of his face, like wet kisses from the clouds that hovered just above his own. Shedding upon him a sense of ecstasy that allowed even his erection access to the cloud filled dream.

The rain began to roll over the rest of his body, trickling upon his temple, neck, shoulder and ribs till he found himself rolling onto his back. So that his belly could be tickled by the tantalizing mist.

"Mmhhh." His head tilting back, absorbed by the cushioning of the cloud, as the cloud above got closer. It's subtle drizzle becoming more pronounced. "Mhhh."

He began to wriggle. The cloud was so close now it almost touched his nose. Mashing itself against him so that he felt cushioned from both sides. Playing centerpiece to a soft marshmallowy sandwich.

"Mhhmn." He jut his hips upward. He wanted to feel more of its softness. Wanted more of its moisture. "More." He whispered. "More."

The cloud became more fog-like, covering his face in a haze, then the haze took on the form of a dense fog that began to fade bit by bit.

"More." He begged once again.

The cloudy haze began to dissipate, the cloud beneath more stable now as he tensed up and realized the haze was a veil created by his half-opened eyelids.

"More." He reached up, eyes opening more as those gorgeous lips came into focus.

He loved Kaleico's lips. Those beautiful lips. Lips that her whole family seemed to possess.

Wait. Her whole family. Grabbing her face he suddenly found full consciousness. In a panic he jerked as his penis began to spew, spilling over onto Zayeda's hand just as she was about to mount him and slip him inside of her.

"What the.." He threw her aside sending her tumbling to the floor. Rolling off the opposite end, grabbing the sheets, wrapping them around his waist. "What..what are you doing in here?"

"I …" She stammered as she stood slowly.

She paused looking at her cum stained palm.

He'd released before she'd had a chance to feel him inside her. Maybe she shouldn't have spent so much time kissing and fondling him? She'd done it wrong. It was her first time and she'd botched it.

In fact, since he never made it inside, she was sure it didn't count ass the 'first time' at all.

"I …" She looked confused. "Didn't you like it?" walking towards him, rounding the bed. "Don't you like me?"

"No!" The words blast from his mouth, louder than planned.

She stopped. Her eyes welled. "Why? What did I … Is it cause I did it wrong?" She stepped towards him. "I'm sorry. Please just.. I promise I can do better."

She pulled the knee length Tee-shirt she wore over her head tossing it aside. For some reason Aaron couldn't take his eyes off her, although he knew he should. She was chiseled and firm. He'd heard that his girlfriend's little sister was a cheerleader, and had spent a bulk of her youth enjoying in activities, ranging from dance to gymnastics, and damn if it hadn't paid off. But not only was she Kaleico's sibling, she was far too young.

"No" He stepped back pressing himself to the wall. "You …" he still couldn't take his eyes away from her. "You gotta..." taking the bed sheet from his waist he leaned forward and wrapped it around her. "You gotta go. You can't be in here." Urging her towards the door.

"I'm sorry. I didn't mean … I was just, I thought you.." She braced the door as he opened it, locking eyes with him. "But I saw you." Cradling his face. "The first day you got here. You looked at me."

He shook his head, wrestling the door open. "No. No. No. I wasn't … you gotta go!"

With no more than a sheet to cover her he shoved her out into a hallway, leaving her to sulk, defeated as she made her way slowly up the stairs. Where she would hide behind the confines of her bedroom door.

·····

Aaron paced the floor. "Jeez!"

He couldn't believe it. What was she thinking? Why would she think that was okay? That it was something he wanted? He didn't understand.

This was the first time in life he'd found himself thanking God for pre-ejaculation. Another second and his dreams of cloud-nine would've turned into a perfect storm of imperfect events.

Images of a pregnant teen and the thought of explaining to Kaleico, why he was the reason for the pregnancy spiraled through his head. There is no way anything he could say would've made sense of such an outcome.

"What the fuck was she thinking!" He asked the empty room once again.

Sitting on the edge of the bed he dropped his head in his lap, stressed beyond all means. Wondering if it was safe to find sleep again.

"I'll be glad when this Christmas shit is over." He shook his head. "I gotta get the hell away from here … sheesh!"

Chapter 19

The wee hours of the a.m. had turned out awkward enough. So much that Aaron hadn't imagined he'd awaken to an increasingly awkward morning. The only thing that could trump a forbidden and embarrassing pre-ejaculation with his girlfriend's sister, was having to look at his girlfriend the morning after. Looking at their mother just magnified the stress. He felt as if a sin was committed, not only against Kaleico but the household itself.

The day started with a wake-up call from Kaleico, which resulted in him declining breakfast. Only to be awakened once again, a few hours later. "Are you running this morning?"

"No." He'd replied, covering his face with a pillow.

As she made an exit it occurred to him. What if Kaleico left to run and her mother also chose to leave for any given reason? He'd be trapped in the house alone with Zayeda.

"Aye." He popped up suddenly. "How about no running at all today? How about, let's just get out of the house."

"Fine. I'll just see what they have planned and we can …"

"No. Just me and you. I could use a little alone time."

"Oh..okay."

No watchful accusing eyes from a suspicious mother. No disturbing glares from a disappointed, or perhaps scorned little sister. No guilt ridden, downcast eyes from Aunt Evelyn, with her oblivious-to all things daughter and debilitated husband in tow. Even Melvin's distant stare would come off as accusatory to a guilt ridden man such as himself today.

And so it went. Without anyone present other than Kaleico he was now able to breathe easy and enjoy her company. Spending a bulk of the day indulging in moments of calm, that didn't call for many words. They'd managed to enjoy a movie, lunch and a carriage ride through downtown Charlotte. In which she'd spent most of her time quiet, with her head nestled on his shoulder.

Afterwards they found themselves enjoying an artsy presentation called 'Christmas

115

Trees Around The World.' A museum exhibit in which trees of all origins were decorated and displayed much to the delight of comer's and goer's, most of whom were paired up like themselves.

When given the option to choose the day's activities he'd purposely chosen things that involved sublime tranquility, over things that required a mutual dialogue, his motivation, fear of spilling the beans. There was something about Kaleico that made men want to give in to urges. Confession being one of them.

After the exhibit they took in a quiet dinner then were on their way home, back to that dreaded house, when Kaleico asked if he minded them stopping at a local retail shop for some last minute odds and ends, to wrap with a bow and place under the tree.

The Wal-Mart was crowded, normal on any day. Walking through the isles he suddenly realized there was room for more conversation than he cared for. Guilt set in again and he found himself feeling as if she were the good cop and he was the suspect under scrutiny. A large bright light overhead while she just smiled and made chit-chat, that would result in him cuffing himself and volunteering to be strapped into a gas filled chamber.

"Aye." He cut her off, not sure what she was saying anyway. "Was that a Best Buy next door?"

"Y..yeah. Why?"

He began to backpedal. "That thing. Remember the thing I was telling you about, for your uncle."

She tried to remember but he continued to explain as he put more space between them.

Already halfway down the aisle he gestured with his hands. "You know. The pad. The program. The Ocular thingamajig." He spoke over his shoulder, disappearing around the corner.

Anything to get out of the store, away from her. Once in Best Buy he made sure to browse the large electronics section till she phoned him from the car, saying she was ready. Purchasing what was deemed the perfect alibi he made his way to the car.

Smiling as he hopped in. "See!"

He pulled a box from the bag that also contained a new I-pad. Explaining to her a bunch of mumbo-jumbo in computer jargon, knowing whenever he talked to her about things of that nature, she'd just get quiet and let him ramble while she blocked him out.

And that's exactly what she did. All the way home.

.....

Back at the house things were somewhat quiet. Kaleico sat on the couch watching television while Sandra busied herself, multi-tasking in the kitchen, handling the stove, a glass of wine and a bit of gossip on her home phone.

Zayeda, held up in her room, descended the stairs long enough to grab a glass of orange juice, and have her mother bombard her with a few rants about undone chores, mid-gossip.

Ignoring Sandra's remarks she mumbled. "Get a smart phone, why don't you." She headed back upstairs, "Who uses a landline anymore?"

"Hold on." Sandra put the caller on hold, pulling the phone from her ear, shouting. "I'm bout to get me a smart ass! That's what I'm bout to get!" putting the phone back to her ear.

"I'm back …. I'm telling you girl, she gonna make me take it back to 1989 on her ass."

She commenced to giggle and gossip. Kaleico was bored. Aaron hadn't come out of the bedroom since they'd returned. She decided to see what he was doing.

The room was dark, except for the desktop lamp, under which he sat prodding at the screen of the newly purchased tablet.

Kaleico entered without knocking. "Hey. You alright?"

"Yeah." He didn't look up. "I'm good." Focused on the tablet. "Just getting this squared away."

She walked over and sat on his lap, pushing the tablet aside. "You're sure you're okay?"

"Yeah." He gave her a kiss. "I'm fine."

"Cause … you've been weird all day.

He paused. Thinking. Finally he said. "Umn … I didn't wanna say anything but … your mom told me about your father."

She got still, quiet. After a second she stood. Folding her arms over her chest she walked to the other side of the room.

119

"Yeah." She uttered. "There's that."

He got up and approached her from behind, wrapping his arms around her waist. "Hey. I'm sorry. I didn't mean to.."

"No. It's okay. I should've told you myself … It's just not something I talk about a lot." She turned around wrapping her arms around his neck. "But I should have told you. I should tell you everything. We..should tell each other everything."

He shrugged. "Yeah. Well some things are just understandable."

She gave him another peck then pulled away. Walking back to the desk, sitting on its edge her hand caressed the I-pad.

"It was hard, seeing him hanging like that. Having to accept that he was … gone."

She explained it a lot like her mother had. Except this time it was coming from her, the girl who owned his heart. This time it was harder to hear.

"Since then I just been … I hate to lose anyone. Anyone at all."

He hugged her. "Don't worry. You'll never lose me. I'll always be her for you. I'll never leave."

This made her hug him back, tight. Looking in his eyes she smiled. "You better not." Pinching his nose. "Or I'd have to kill you myself."

They laughed, gazing into one another's eyes.

She changed the subject. "You know we're gonna have to go in there and eat again, right? Cause if I tell my momma we had dinner while we were out, lord have mercy on both of us!"

"I think I can make a little room for something extra."

"Well if you know Sandra that's exactly what you better do!"

She walked towards the door, pulling him along as she led the way.

Chapter 20

Zayeda heard her mother calling from downstairs, dinner was ready. Stepping away from the bedroom window she shouted that she'd be down in a moment, then returned to the window, peering across the back lawn. Frowning when she saw the shadow, in the adjacent house, standing behind closed curtains.

Holding her phone waist high she text: why did u close them?

She watched the shadow as it text back: put it on.

Why? She replied, the glow from the phone illuminating her bare breast as she continued: why wont u look?

Youre not ready yet. #18 in a few months

Look!

No

They'll look the same a few months from now #just look! #why don't you see me?

I do SMH But not like this: not yet

Why cant you just see me #NOW ##I'm not a little girl anymore #I want you to touch me

. . . . .

Chavis stood behind the closed curtains, breathing heavily. Zayeda's half-naked silhouette calling to him as he read her message.

I want you to touch me

Before he could reply, another message followed.

Like he did

Chavis' brow furrowed. Snatching the curtain back his chest heaved at the sight of her explicit breast, nostrils flaring he text in reply:

Like who?

.....

Zayeda smiled as the curtains parted. She could see his eyes now, glued to her flesh. Inhaling deeply her breast swelled and begged to be handled.

She read his message: Like who?

A sly grin on her face, she had his attention. Now all she had to do was   keep it.

.....

Chavis' phone blipped in reply, foam forming in the corners of his mouth, fuming as he read.

@Aaron

Chapter 21

Aaron had slept much better than the night before. Perhaps this could be attributed to the lack of sleep the previous night. Whatever the case he'd made his way to the bedroom last night, after stuffing himself with Sandra's latest culinary delight. Not wanting to let on that he'd already ate, he had two servings, turning him into a hibernating grizzly. Falling asleep instantly once he'd left the table and hit the mattress.

His 'dream girl's' presence at the table hadn't unnerved him, as much as mere thoughts of her had managed to do throughout that day. Maybe he had been too tired to care?

While he was out like a light, Kaleico had spent the remainder of the evening chatting it up with her mother. While Zayeda kept to herself watching T.V. from the living room couch, until soon they all made their way to bed. Kaleico in her mother's room just like all the nights before.

The morning sun welcomed him back to the living. Stretching his arms his hands broke the beams of light that set the wall aglow.

Pancakes seemed to be the house special. He'd be sure to let Kaleico know, he'd now grown accustomed to being awakened by the smell of syrup and hot cakes in the morning. She'd now have to take on the task of catering to his newfound love of breakfast in the morning.

This would definitely be a topic of discussion before their return home.

Grabbing a few items he exited the room and shuffled up the stairs. He'd been there long enough to gain his bearings and feel free to navigate the floors of the home without hand holding.

A luke warm shower and fifteen minutes later he emerged with a smile on his face, waltzing towards the kitchen, following the scent of strawberries and maple, feet dancing to the clank of forks and plates calling his name.

"Good morning, everyone." His voice entered the room before he did.

"Good morning." The replying voice more masculine than his ears were prepared to receive.

He stopped short, his smile almost falling to a straight line, but he quickly revived the corners and upward contour of his mouth when he saw Kaleico, her sister and mother at the table as well.

He noted Chavis had taken a seat at the head of the table, Sandra at the opposite end. Kaleico opposite her sister, who sat at the end closest to Sandra while she sat close to Chavis.

There was an open seat on Zayeda's side but no spare seat on the side Kaleico sat on.

"Good morning." The ladies added their two cents.

Chavis stood, sliding the chair out to his left, so Aaron could fill the gap between he and Zayeda.

"Thanks" Aaron grabbed the seat.

Everyone watched as he lift the chair and walked around to Kaleico's side, urging her to slide down to her mother's end, wedging himself between she and Chavis. Once seated he gave Kaleico a kiss on the cheek.

Aaron looked down the table. "So Sandra." He stopped, snapping his finger as an afterthought, he reached over and grabbed the plate that had been prepared and ready in his presumed spot. Looking to Sandra again. "I was just thinking" he took a bite and spoke as he chewed. "How great it would be if, before we left," he swallowed then grabbed Kaleico's hand planting a kiss on it before finishing. "If you would teach this woman, the love of my life, how to make these world class pancakes!"

Sandra blushed. "Well you know. The secret's not in the pancakes." She gyrated in her seat. "That's where a lot of women get it wrong.

Cause the cakes ain't nothing if the syrup ain't right and ready!"

She gushed over his praise, much to Chavis' dismay. He didn't like the way she smiled at Aaron. Nor did he like the way Zayeda stole glances at Aaron then cut her eye at him in disdain.

Chavis shifted attention to Kaleico, sitting with Aaron's hand in her own. Then Chavis saw her look to him, the words "does this make you jealous?" Oozing from her lips in a slow, syrupy slurr.

Chavis stiffened staring off into space.

"Chavis?" Kaleico snapped her fingers. "Didn't you hear me?"

"Yeah .. yeah." He became coherent. "You asked me if ..." what had she asked? "If I ..."

She finished for him. "If you already knew the secret to momma's syrup?"

"Oh." He must have been hallucinating. "I didn't. She never shared it with me."

Sandra shrugged. "Well I've never shared it with anybody. Last person I shared my secret syrup with was yall's father."

129

Aaron urged. "How else can she make me the happiest man on earth." He clasped his hands together. "Please Miss Sandra, you have to tell her."

Sandra paused. Pursing her lips she sat her juice down and got up out of her seat. "You know what?"

Making her way to Aaron, leaning over his shoulder she cupped her hand and whispered something.

Aaron smiled as she whispered. "Oh. Okay." He cut an eye at Chavis, giving him a wink. "So that's the secret!"

She leaned away and spoke aloud. "Are you kidding me? You think it got that good, without a little more work than that?" She shook her head. "No sweety. There's much more to Sandra's syrup than that!"

Leaning forward she began to whisper behind a cupped hand once again.

Aaron nodded. "Of course. Of course. WOWW! I never would've thought it."

Sandra slapped him on the shoulder as she straightened up. "You better recognize!" She snapped her fingers and whipped her hair, sashaying back to her seat. "I mean it. You better not tell nobody."

Kaleico looked at her and asked. "Well. How am I supposed to do it if you telling him, not to tell anyone how to make it?" She shook her head, facing Aaron. "I told you she was crazy."

"Crazy?" Sandra humph'd. "Girl I just gave your man the secret to making a pancake, he crave so much, he'll get up and make them his self." Whipping her hair again. "And while he stacking those cakes in the morning, cooking for himself, guess who else he gonna make sure get a few on her plate?"

Kaleico raised her hand for a high five. "Lady I like the way you think!"

Sandra high fived. "Now that's how you get a man to give you breakfast in bed." She popped her collar. "Why beg him when all you gotta do is give him a sample of that good syrup!" She wiggled in her seat. "Then teach him how to whip it himself. Till it's just ... like ... you like it!"

They high fived again. Kaleico turned and gave him a kiss. "Breakfast in bed, huh? I can live with that!"

Zayeda cut her eyes at Chavis. Snarling her nose she then turned to Aaron and spoke. "If I could be so lucky."

Kaleico looked at her and assured. "One day sweety. One day."

Zayeda could've done without her input. Sandra's voice was a more welcomed consolation. Even though the words were the same.

"One day, sweety." Her mother reassured. "Be patient."

Zayeda smirked. "Why be patient, when you can be proactive."

"Listen to my baby using those big words." Sandra gave her a high five this time. "Proactive! My baby said that!"

This time even Zayeda had to laugh. In fact the only person at the table who wasn't laughing, nor smiling, was Chavis.

.....

After breakfast Chavis made it a priority to shoulder aside Aaron's offer to help Sandra with the dishes. "I got it." He joined her by the sink before Aaron could get to her.

It was no inconvenience to Aaron. It was time for he and Kaleico's morning run. Zayeda already long gone had convinced her mother to lend her the car. "In the spirit of Christmas." Miraculously Sandra caved with the condition she return in no less than three to four hours, car unscathed.

The clock started before the words were out of her mouth. Zayeda was halfway out of the driveway before the sentence was completed.

Already dressed in full running attire Aaron was all too happy to hear the words. "You ready?" as Kaleico round the corner.

Tired of Chavis' over the shoulder glares he was more than ready to leave. "Ready!"

Kaleicos' running pants held her rear high and tight. "Good. Cause we gotta do a little extra today. Make up for the day we missed!"

Aaron eyed his watch. "So we talking, bout an hour, hour and a half?"

"Why not make it two?" She challenged.

He entertained. "Let's do it."

Sandra turned from the sink to weigh in. "Two hours! I don't even like to drive that long, much less run! Have fun. Lord knows I wouldn't."

Aaron and Kaleico laughed. Waving goodbye they made an exit, leaving Sandra and Chavis to themselves and dish duty.

Sandra towel dried the dishes, Chavis handled the wash and rinse, listening to her ramble about gifts she needed to purchase before the holiday. He continued to work without much input on the matter. Finally the last glass was done, drying it off she placed it in the rack then walked over to wipe down the kitchen table.

Chavis turned his back to the counter, leaning against it, while he watched her perform the task. "So. Why you never showed me?"

Sandra, leaning across the table now, looked back over her shoulder. "Never showed you what, Chavis?"

"Your pancakes. The secret?"

She chuckled. Still halfway across the table, one leg hovering the floor. "Boy. As long as you been enjoying them I thought you didn't care."

"Of course I care. I care about everything, when it comes to you."

She turned placing a hand on her hip, smiling. "Awe. You're such a sweetheart." She faced the table again, speaking without looking. "I told yall. It ain't about the cakes." She unconsciously did the same gyrating dip she did earlier, except this time there was no seat to hold her rear as it jiggled about. "The secrets in the syrup!"

He watched her. Licking his lips as she wiped the table. "Show me."

"Show you? Boy what you.." Sandra turned and found him extremely close to her. So close that she would've toppled over, if not for the table propping her backside.

He stepped closer. "You said it's deeper than the cakes." Pressing his flesh against her. "Show me."

The sensation of his hands, caressing her rear took her by surprise. Heaving a sigh of anxiety her lips parted. "Chavis. What are you.."

"Show me the secret." He leaned his face towards hers. "The syrup behind the cakes." Gripping her ass tighter now.

The slap echoed through the kitchen. Staggering backwards he grabbed his cheek.

Sandra had reacted off pure reflex.

"Chavis. Baby I'm sorry. I just don't understand. Why? Why would you.."

Lunging forward he cut her words short when he shoved her back onto the table then whirled her around towards the sink.

Using her hands for leverage, Sandra shoved herself backwards, sending them stumbling towards the wall.

Grabbing her waist, he shifted momentum so that her back met the wall, just by the doorframe with a thud. Pressing her flush he held her chin steady, jaw agape, cutting off her air as he aggressively forced his tongue deep down into her mouth.

.....

Only ten minutes into their jog, their pace had allowed them to cover quite a distance. Kaleico was fast and also competitive. Aaron knew that she was trying to take a pace that would make him cry uncle and tap out, a feat she'd yet to pull off. Looking over at her he smiled deciding today he would be the aggressor. Speeding up he took off, leaving her with no other words than the ones printed on the back of his shirt.

"Oh yeah?" She quipped, accelerating until she held a slight lead.

He spoke in a gasp. "You really think you're gonna make two hours at this pace?"

"Why?" Her breathing was steady, controlled. "Can't handle it?"

He shrugged, picking up speed but she remained neck in neck. "I can do this all day."

"All day it is!" She fired back.

A loud blaring sound from his wristwatch jarred his mind. "Dammit!"

As soon as he heard the notification he remembered. An interview, a conference call, set to be made at a certain calendar date and time, logged into his watch as a reminder. Coming to an immediate halt, resting his hands on his knees he caught his breath.

Kaleico, realizing he stopped, slowed to a crawl then back pedaled. "What's wrong? A cramp?"

He shook his head, showing her his watch. "I forgot I had something important ... I need to get to a phone."

She shrugged. "Wish I could help you bud, but real runners leave the phone at home. Guess you're gonna have to book it to the house!"

He nod in agreement. "Yeah. You're right. I'm sorry to spoil.."

"Oh." Kaleico laughed. "You think cause your run is over, mine is over?" She pat him on the back then leaned in for a kiss on the cheek. "Catch you back at the house."

She produced a key and passed it to him. No sooner than the door key touched his palm she jetted away, much faster than before, her way of letting him know he'd slowed her down all long.

Aaron laughed at the gesture. Looking at his watch he was glad he'd set the notification to alert him slightly ahead of time. He had at least ten minutes, which meant he'd have to push it back to the house, opting for a speed much faster than that which carried him to this point.

"If only she could see how fast I *really* am!" He took off in the opposite direction heading back to the house.

Chapter 22

The driveway came into view. Aaron checked his watch, pleased to see he had a few minutes to spare. Just enough to take pause in order to catch his breath.

Squatting down he let one palm rest on his knee while the other held the ground. Stretching out to a push-up position, easing into an upward facing dog pose, rolling back to a downward dog. Holding for three breaks he raised and lowered his heels, loosening his calves before thrusting his knees forward, landing back in a squatted position.

Rising slowly arms stretched to the sky, flexing his shoulder's he walked to the door and took the key from his pocket, letting himself inside.

The living room and kitchen were empty. A loud bump caught his ear. Stopping for a second he looked around then continued towards his bed area to get his phone.

Entering the bedroom he searched for the phone, when another bump came from above. This time the sound came through the vent.

"Unh..Please. Please."

The low murmuring plea was followed by a low thud, then another, this time louder, harder. Next came a flurry of bumps alongside a ghastly gasp.

It didn't sound good at all. Running to the kitchen he grabbed the first thing he saw, a long carving blade poised in the knife rack. Yanking it free he began a slow creep up the stairs, until a shriek made him speed up.

Taking the steps two at a time he reached the top, running towards the sound. Knowing it had come from the vent, by way of Kaleico's old room he made haste towards the partially open door.

A gurgling sound came from the room. A female's voice, low and desperate. Raising the blade he got against the wall peering around the corner.

The blade fell from his grip. The light thud it made when it hit the carpet wasn't enough to be heard above the whimpering cries that now became loud ranting screams.

"Please ... oh. Please don't stop. Please don't ... ohmn.. Oh god. Chavis. Omn..God that feels so good."

Aaron stood there frozen. Sandra's back was to him, her ass exposed, Chavis' hands

141

cupping it, while her legs held firm, wrapped around his waist. Arms around his neck for support she held on for dear life.

It was clear, Chavis' strong arms and the peg he called his manhood was more than enough to keep her from falling. Bucking his hips sending her bouncing with each thrust, his testicles swung forward as she fell back down onto the deep planted root inside her. Assuring that, no matter how high he bounced her she wouldn't meet the floor, as long as his long hard flesh was there to catch her, and keep her levitating above the surface.

"Oh God. Oh God!"

Her cries of agonizing pleasure were like fingernails on chalkboards to Aaron's ears.

Chavis' eyes locked with his. He stood there bouncing her up and down, a menacing smile on his face he winked at Aaron and began to unleash a domineering series of violent thrust that made her head roll and whirl with passion.

"Awoow … ow .. ohhh!" She began to clench him tight, trying to restrict the amount of penetration administered.

Her body was confused. The more she hurt the more she wanted. The more she wanted to cry the more she felt overwhelmed with joy.

142

Until finally she began to submit to all of those feelings at once.

She began to shake, crying and moaning as she babbled and held him close. Chavis stood there holding her at bay until she was able to sustain herself. Eyes locked on Aaron all the while.

Aaron couldn't believe it. He regressed slowly stepping out of view as Chavis allowed Sandra's feet to fall to the floor.

He'd seen more than enough. Running down the stairs Aaron bee lined to the bedroom to grab his phone before heading for the front door. Just as he stepped out to exit he began to hear the headboard creaking and Sandra's screams become more prominent, so much they seemed to chase him out the door.

Clutching the phone in his hand he found himself at a full on sprint. A conference call the furthest thing from his mind.

.....

Chavis rolled off of Sandra's backside. He admired every inch of her. Even at her age. Just like Evelyn she was still firm all over. Good

143

genetics were obviously a family treasure, and as he just found out some good things went far beyond the exterior.

Sandra expressed disbelief, questioning her own actions. "Oh my God." Then repeated in celebratory praise. "Oh my God."

She rolled over, not knowing what to say, staring at him. He lay there quietly her head on his chest, waiting for her to say what she was thinking.

"I.. I wanna say that I shouldn't have." She cradled his chin. "But every part of me feels like.." her hand eased down his chest then his stomach till it found his shaft. "Like I was supposed to have done it..all along."

Loosening her grip on his rod she pushed it away like it was an object of sin.

Rolling on her side, facing away from him she teared up as she added. "I hope this changes nothing. The way you view me, I mean?"

Reaching over her waist he took her hand, whispering in her ear. "I love you. I've always loved you." His breath danced on her neck. "I'll always love you."

He thought to himself.

Every single one of you.

Chapter 23

Kaleico, full trot, bent the corner only to see Aaron, barreling towards her with long hard strides.

She smiled. He'd obviously gone out of his way to make sure, he'd got as much of a run in as he could, even after running home to make that call.

Slowing her step she worked her way to a stationary pause, running in place as he approached. "Well. Well. Well." She continued to bounce about. "Missed me, huh?"

His breathing was intense, labored, struggling to get his words out he began to hyperventilate as he fell back on his haunches.

Kaleico stopped. "Babe. What's wrong!" She knelt beside him. "Wait a minute. Just calm down. Breathe. Breathe. Breathe. There you go..breathe. Nice and slow. Niice and sloow."

She coached him to a state of calm, giving him a moment to gather himself, then she asked again.

"Are you okay? What's wrong? You look like you're running from the devil."

If the devil was, any and everything to do with her family. He was.

"Aaron. What is it? What's got you worked up?"

"I..I gotta tell you…tell you something."

She rubbed his back. "Well, you got my attention."

She helped him to his feet. "I'm listening. Tell me. What is it?"

"Your … your.." His phone buzzed, he suddenly thought about the important call, the interview. He'd forgot "Dammit!"

"What?" She asked as he spun away and looked at his phone.

He was sure they were calling to ask what happened. But it wasn't them. It was a message, an email attachment with Chavis' name on it. Opening the message, his eyes got big.

"Baby?" Kaleico touched his shoulder.

He jumped and with a few quick taps to the screen shut off his phone.

She asked. "What is it? Did something go wrong

with the job?"

"Yea..un..no." He shook his head. "I was just trying to tell you." Giving her a forced smile.

"They seemed to like what I had to say ... said things look promising."

"Oh sweety." She wrapped herself around him. "That's great! Come on. We gotta get you home. We have to celebrate!"

"Well" He stalled. "I mean they didn't say I got it. Just said it looks good. That's all."

"Hey." She grabbed his face. "We've popped bottles for no reason at all. Why not for hope's sake?" She winked. "Besides you were excited enough to run to meet me, like a bat outta hell. Something worth running for is worth jumping up and down for, right?"

"Yeah." Another forced smile. "You're right." Clasping her hand. "But how about we just take our time and walk the rest of the way?"

She mulled it over then resigned.

"Hmmmn? Well I guess I could take the easy way out." She started to walk. "Just this time."

.....

Chavis looked at the message on his screen. A reply from Aaron.

Fuck you

He laughed again after reading it for the fourth time. Aaron clearly hadn't liked the message Chavis had sent. A photo taken by Chavis their first night out. Two photo's in fact: One from the food court at the mall, when he'd taken Aaron's phone from the Candy Crush girl, and the other from the drunken spree at the strip club.

He was sure Aaron was so hammered he didn't remember having the girl at the club perform any of the acts in the pictures, but it didn't matter if he remembered. All that mattered was his memory had been jogged now.

He'd sent Aaron the pic's, with the caption. "Go head tell her # I dare you"

. . . . .

Aaron sat alone in the bedroom, scrolling through the pic's again. Kaleico was upstairs in the shower. Her mother had just walked by minutes ago when he'd stepped out to grab something from the kitchen.

A robe and towel on her head, Sandra had clearly freshened up. Oblivious to the fact he'd witnessed the whole ordeal.

Truth was since stepping off the plane he'd witnessed far more than he could take in such a short stay. The sooner Christmas came the better, he was ready to leave. Ready to get as far away from Charlotte as possible. ASAP!

Once again he'd found himself held up in the room for a bulk of the day. A stomach virus, he'd told Kaleico when she'd come to check on him. Using the down time to fumble around a bit more with the I-pad he'd purchased, hoping to have the intended feature programmed and operable by nights end.

Doing something special for someone in such dire need as Kaleico's uncle, Melvin, would be the only good thing to come from this holiday excursion turned nightmare.

Hours later, once again Kaleico came knocking. She'd brought him a bowl of soup at lunch time. Now she insisted he come out and get something hearty in his stomach.

The pit of his gut growled, daring him to decline. He was starving. Enough was enough.

"Okay." He gave in. "Just let me hop in the shower real quick and I'll be out in a minute."

Without dispute she closed the door. Aaron grabbed a pair of boxer's from his bag. Stepping out into the hall he spotted Zayeda, sitting on the couch with her back to him as she watched television. Yet another reason he couldn't wait to get away from this house.

She'd leaned forward squinting at the T.V. "Dag!' She commented. "People are crazy!"

Aaron was about to walk up the stairs but this made him stop and look at the screen. It was a news report. The bi-line read.

Man Found Dead.

Zayeda turned up the volume.

"Police say there's no doubt this was a violent display of aggravated murder." The camera only showed a portion of the victim, his head was blurred out. *"Images are too heinous to display. Unconfirmed sources say the young male, a worker at this restaurant, slash bar suffered fatal injuries to the head, neck and ..."*

The bar. It was the one they'd visited, the one with the ugly sweater party. And the victim, though his face was blurred there was something all too familiar about his shirt.

Shrugging the thought away he ran up the steps. Ready to hit the shower, so he could eat and put an end to another awful, and awe filled day.

Chapter 25

Christmas Eve, finally. As far as Aaron was concerned the only thing worth celebrating more than Jesus' birthday was the fact it was almost over. The trip, the holiday, all of it. Today was just a day away from one last supper and a long awaited goodbye. *Nice to meet you. Hope to never see you, any of you ever, ever again.*

The day seemed to move in a blur, shopping, dealing with hectic lines at the mall, Aaron felt adrift all the while. Contemplating if he should come clean and tell Kaleico everything. He'd already avoided hurting her, with accusations about her Aunt Evelyn and Chavis but they were just that, assumptions. But this thing with her mother was concrete.

He wondered how long it'd been going on. It didn't matter. He couldn't exactly fault Sandra for wanting to get her rocks off, but he didn't like the way Chavis played himself up to Kaleico as the innocent family friend. She needed to know, the guy who was 'like her brother' was actually scum in disguise.

But the pictures Chavis messaged him had caused him to refrain, what if she didn't care about his mental capacity, what if just seeing them was enough to make her leave him forever?

Surely their love was deeper than that. Surely she'd trust his word and believe him, over that creep, the creep who smiled in her face and fucked her mother as soon as her back was turned.

Not only did he want to leave, he also wanted to get Kaleico away from these crazy people, all of them as soon as possible. Her sister, mother, Aunt, the family friend, as far as he could tell her cousin was the only one that hadn't screwed her over.

It was senseless. Kaleico loved her family and was clueless to the fact none of them were worthy of her heartfelt affection.

He'd done well to contain himself the entire day. Walking through the mall with her mother, her sister everyone smiling and chatting it up with the only person in the family, his girl, who wasn't carrying on like a backstabbing harlot.

Daylight had come to past and the moon held high. Glad to be back at the house he smiled, his first smile of the day, brought on by the sight of Kaleico's uncle, Melvin, as they entered the house. Next to him his daughter, Chantelle. Evelyn was nowhere in sight.

Sandra entered with bags in hand. "Hey. I didn't know yall were here. Where's the van?"

"Oh." Chantelle answered. "Ma went to pick up some stuff around the corner, at Chavis' house."

Aaron noticed how Sandra's eyes downcast at the mention of Chavis' name. Her reaction was much like her sisters'- Kaleicos'

Aunt Evelyn- whenever she and Chavis were in the same room.

And true to form, the mention of his name sent Melvin into a slobbering series of grunts and bobs. Aaron wondered if he was the only one who noticed this?

Zayeda set her bags down, Aaron caught the intentional saunter as she brushed by giving him the eye.

He looked for an excuse to leave the room. "Uncle Melvin!" Walking over he looked to Chantelle and gestured towards her father. "Do you mind?"

She smiled. "No. I.."

"I have something I wanna show him." Aaron unlocked the wheels on Melvin's chair. "A gift." He shrugged. "Why make him wait? Christmas is only hours away. At the strike of twelve, technically."

Chantelle nodded. "Sure."

Aaron wheeled him towards the bedroom as Kaleico called behind him. "You boy's be sure to put your toys up when you're done."

"Ha Ha!" Aaron looked back then entered the room, closing the door behind him.

Pushing Melvin by the desk he turned the lamp on and pulled up a seat, taking the pad from its box he began to explain its function.

He couldn't tell if Melvin was staring intently at the screen, or just off into space. His eyes were open, that was close to a sign he was paying attention, Aaron guessed?

After a long-winded explanation he activated it, so that the display screen illuminated Melvin's face. A series of letters and pre-set phases appeared.

"All you have to do is focus on the letter you want to use and this thing." He pointed to a small accessory attached to one of the ports. "Will recognize your ocular reactions and like magic." He snapped his fingers "your words will print right here."

He looked to be sure Melvin was listening. Melvin did nothing to confirm the fact.

"Wanna try it?"

Melvin appeared to focus. At least Aaron thought so. He sat there waiting, holding the pad for him. Maybe the program was a sack of bull, maybe he was being foolish?

A blip on the screen made Aaron perk up. It was one word, a perfect phrase.

Hello.

"Look!" Aaron was excited. "Is that … did you do that, or is this thing short circuiting?"

NO NO NO

Another preset phrase registered, repeatedly. Then after a long pause, one sole letter appeared.

M, then another letter E

"ME!" Aaron read. "Me. You, It's you. It's working!"

He jumped from his seat and ran towards the door, so he could tell everyone, then he stopped. He thought about something. Walking back to Melvin he knelt beside the wheelchair.

"I" Aaron began. "There's something I wanna ask you." He paused, thinking it through. "It may be my imagination but I notice, every time a certain name is mentioned around you, you go Ape-shit!"

He stopped. Ape shit may be an offensive choice of words to a cripple, who could be simply convulsing at random moments, falsely attributed to the mention of a name.

He waited then asked. "Chavis? Am I right?"

This time Melvin didn't so much as tremor. There was Aaron's answer. He was wrong, he'd made an ass of himself. Probably offended him.

"I'm sorry … Let me…" The screen flashed. A blip. A single letter.

C

A moment passed. Another letter appeared H…Another moment, another letter…
A.

Aaron watched as Melvin struggled to tilt his head forward, the pad had been left to rest on his lap. His eyes searching for the right letters.

"Fella's!" The voice made Aaron cringe. Turning around he saw Chavis standing behind him.

He didn't hear him enter.

Chavis wore a devious grin. Crossing the room he toyed with items on the dresser. "So tell me, what yall boys in here doing?" he nudged shoulders with Aaron as he passed. "In here all to yourselves."

He eyed Melvin then Aaron. Watching Aaron for an uncomfortable moment then joked.

"Let me guess. Yall were having a conversation!" he laughed.

"Man Get the fuck outta here!" Aaron barked through gritted teeth in a low hush.

He noticed Melvin's shakes and grunts had suddenly reappeared. Coincidence? He doubted it.

Chavis held Aaron's eyes at a stare as he reached over and placed a hand on Melvin's shoulder. "Ol' Melvin here gets worked up round me." That smile again. "Don't think he likes me much."

Melvin's eyes twitched and danced about.

Chavis continued to taunt. "You know, Aaron. Me and you, we could play nice. Just till it's time for you to leave."

"I got a better idea." Aaron shot in reply. "How about we just stay outta each other's way till Christmas is passed, and me and Kaleico can leave all this shit in the wind. Never to return again!" This time it was he who smirked. "Trust me. You won't be receiving an invite to the wedding. Did I tell you?" He pulled a ring from his pocket. "I'm thinking about popping the question."

He could see Chavis' heart crumble. Take that.

Chavis lunged forward, grabbing his collar. "What makes you think I won't go in there right now and show her these pictures? One glance at these and she'll be begging me to shove that ring down your throat, and escort your ass ten thousand feet away from here!"

Aaron broke free of his grip and shoved him away. "Fuck those pictures! I'm sure, you fucking her mom trumps that! Think about it. Not only will it hurt Kaleico, but her mother as well."

Chavis chuckled. Turning his back as if walking away, then whirling around back to face him. "Well I guess that means, you still got me beat on the shit list." He got in Aaron's face. "Considering you fucked her little..." stressing the last word "Sister!"

Aaron's expression fell flat. He tried to regain his poise but it was too late. "What ... wha ... we..I never screwed with her sis.."

"That's not what she said."

Chavis showed him his phone. Aaron only saw a few key words.

Touch me like he did.

Like who did?

Chavis smiled. "Yeah." Knocking the ring from Aaron's hand to the floor. "That's what I thought!"

Aaron bent to retrieve it as Chavis circled him.

"You see. This is how it's gonna go. You'll be going home early. No need in hanging around for New Year's."

He wanted to assure him, New Year's never was an option to begin with but Chavis didn't let him speak.

"Thing is Kaleico want be going with you." Chavis pointed out. "She'll be too mad about the fight yall had. The one you're gonna start, intentionally. Giving reason to subtract yourself from this equation of ours." He pat him on the shoulder. "She'll get over it. I'll make sure of that. By New Year's she'll be celebrating and cutting her loses, ready to start anew. And you, you'll be old news."

"What makes you think I'd choose to.."

"What makes you think you have a choice?" He flashed his phone, the pictures and Zayeda's message again. "Just go in there, enjoy tonight, enjoy tomorrow. Have a little

Christmas dinner, you're more than welcome to join us. But after that I want you gone. Gone for good."

Melvin began to shake and grunt aggressively. So much that the pad fell from his lap and lodged itself between his hip and the side panel of the wheelchair.

Chavis turned to Melvin, toying with him. "What's that you say?" he grabbed the back of the chair. "I think he's ready to get back in there with the rest of the family."

Melvin continued to jerk and grunt as Chavis began to push him towards the door. Leaving Aaron to ponder his ultimatum.

Chapter 26

Midnight came fast. It was typical in Kaleico's household for everyone to open one of their gifts at midnight then others in the morning. However this holiday prequel sometimes resulted in all gifts being opened at once.

Aaron numbed himself with spiked eggnog, enjoying every soft little kiss planted on his cheek, basking in every hug Kaleico gave him. All the while knowing he couldn't stand the thought of these being his last.

He had to do something. What? He didn't know. But something had to be done.

Chavis handed Kaleico a box. "Here."

Everyone watched as she opened it. Her eyes widened and she giggled embarrassingly as she pulled the skimpy negligee from the box. "Chavis …"

"What?" He smiled. "I see how you two stay pawing at one another. It's a two in one. A gift for both of you." He shrugged. "I figured it was the cheapest way to kill two birds."

Kaleico held it against her, letting it drape over her frame, turning to Aaron. "For the both of us." She winked, giving him a peek at the thong that remained in the box.

Aaron urged a smile. Knowing this was Chavis' way of implying that this was attire he would never see, something Chavis himself intended to see her waltzing around in. He knew Chavis had eyes for Kaleico, it was clear he had eyes for them all. Every woman in the house.

Aaron didn't say much for the next hour. 1 a.m. came and he finally left his spot on the couch, only to give Chantelle a hand loading her father into the van. They buckled him in as Chavis and Kaleico followed Evelyn out of the house, helping her carry a few things.

Placing the bags in the back Evelyn thanked them all, and joined Chantelle who already sat up front in the passenger's seat with the engine running.

"Bye, everybody!" Chantelle rolled the window down a crack.

They pulled out of the driveway. Kaleico at Aaron's side, fingers interlocked used her free hand to wave goodbye as they drove off.

Aaron turned to kiss Kaleico on the cheek. That's when his eyes locked with Chavis' who slithered to the other side of her meeting the other side of her face with a kiss of his own.

Sandwiched between them she smiled. Aaron could feel the chill bumps forming on her arm, they did this whenever he aroused her. Problem was at the moment he didn't know who they were forming for.

"Aaron." She cut her eyes at him. "You better stop before my momma look out the door and see you."

"Wha.." Aaron started then stopped when he saw Chavis' hand retracting from her ass cheek.

Aaron looked down at his own hand, as if to make sure it wasn't his own palm that did the deed. His hand reaffirmed by bawling itself into a fist and before he knew it, had shoved Kaleico aside and leapt towards Chavis, with a flying right to the jaw.

The loud crack made Kaleico flinch as if she'd been hit. Catching her balance, after the shove, she quickly realized what happened.

Aaron followed the punch with a hard left that Chavis managed to steer clear of. The momentum of the punch sent Aaron reeling to the ground. He quickly worked his way back to his feet.

"Aaron!" Kaleico yelled.

He rushed head first into Chavis' gut. "You sonofabitch, I'm gonna"

Chavis locked his arm around his shoulder and twist him in a spiraling heap to the ground.

"Aaron stop!" Kaleico cried out. "Ma!" calling for help as she tried to separate the two.

Aaron was now on top, pounding Chavis' face with all the might he could channel. "I'll fuckin kill you! You hear me, you fuckin.."

She'd never seen him act or talk like this before. "Ma. Help!"

Just as the front door opened Kaleico grabbed Aaron's elbow, mid-swing, and the jerk reaction sent her falling backwards on her ass.

Sandra stepped out just in time to see Aaron send her daughter to the ground. "What the hell is going on out here?"

She ran out and tried to stop the melee. Aaron still swinging furiously ended up knocking her off balance as well.

"Aaron!" Kaleico cried out again. "Aaron! Why?"

Aaron drew back and froze at the sound of her cry. He'd blacked out. He didn't understand how he'd got to the ground. Why was Chavis under him with a bleeding nose and lip?

Chavis looked up at him, his teeth blood stained he whispered. "Looks like you came up with an exit strategy, after all." He smiled. "Good shot."

"Fuck you!"

Aaron dropped a double fisted blow that made Chavis close his eyes and keep them closed.

This time both Kaleico and Sandra pushed Aaron off of him.

"Aaron. Have you lost your mind!" Kaleico looked at him with disappointment and disbelief then knelt beside Chavis.

She and her mother tapping on his face. "Wake up. Chavis, are you okay?"

Chavis lay behind closed eyes, listening. Ignoring the taps on the cheek till he was satisfied they'd bought his act.

"Unnh." He groaned. "Wh..what happened?" His eyes fluttered.

Kaleico jumped to her feet, shoving Aaron she cursed. "What the fuck is wrong with you? Why would you do that?"

"I.." He struggled. "The guy's an asshole!" He had a million good reasons, none of which he wished to disclose.

She shoved him again. "I can't believe you! This my mother's house, Aaron! My mother's house and you do this?"

Sandra helped Aaron to his feet, throwing his arm over her shoulder. Kaleico ran over and took the other arm. Both of them lugged him towards the house.

"No." Chavis stopped them, taking his arm from their shoulders. "I'm good." He rubbed his jaw.

Aaron stood by watching. Noticing for the first time, Zayeda was standing in the door, looking at everything as it unfolded.

Chavis wiped away the blood with his sleeve and spit at the ground. "I'm alright. Don't worry. I just wanna get back to the house and call it a night."

Kaleico protested. "Well let me take you. You can't walk like this."

He shook his head, putting on a limp as he headed towards the side of the house. "I only gotta cut through the backyard." He cut an eye at Aaron as he finished. "I tore the fence down, remember?"

She'd forgotten.

He added. "There's nothing between us anymore. Easy access."

He disappeared around the house, leaving Aaron in the front yard with accusing eyes piercing through him. All except Zayeda who stood in the doorway smiling, giving him a big thumbs up.

Aaron started towards them. "Sandra. I'm sorry. I.." he faced Kaleico. "Baby please let me expla.."

"Aaron, I can't take this shit!" Kaleico backed away, turning on her heels she ran to the house "Maybe you should just go!"

"But baby, let's talk.."

She stopped at the door, looking back. "Talk to me when I return to Chicago. Right now I just wanna be here and have a nice, perfect visit with my family. That's all I wanted." She cried. "Not this!"

Pushing past her sister she ran up the stairs and went to her mother's room, slamming the door.

"Sandra." Aaron pleaded.

Folding her arms, Sandra shook her head and walked away.

Aaron dropped his head and moved towards the door, brushing past Zayeda, who whispered. "We still got us."

That was it. He'd had enough. Going to the room, he'd called his own, he grabbed the phone and googled the number for the nearest hotel and a cab to take him there.

Dialing the number he spoke. "Yes. I'd like to have a cab."

Chapter 27

Chantelle helped Evelyn get her father out of the van. Wheeling him inside she made small talk with her mother, who's thoughts seemed elsewhere.

Evelyn was frustrated. She'd signaled Chavis that she wanted to spend a moment with him tonight, planning to double back once her husband was situated, and her daughter fast asleep. A sure fate after cups of eggnog, Evelyn herself had coaxed her to drink.

But Chavis had replied with an inconspicuous shake of the head. "No." Evelyn was furious. He knew that she wanted him, needed him inside her. It was the least he could have done. It was Christmas. Wasn't she worthy of a little yule tide log.

"Asshole." She cursed under her breath, yanking her wig off her head as she entered her bedroom, leaving her daughter to tend to Melvin alone.

Her best wig, tightest dress, sexiest snowflake flecked leggings and he had the audacity to decline! Who was he to deny her what she wanted, what she needed so badly?

She feared her favorite toy, or straddling her husband's face just wouldn't do for the night. But now it appeared to be her only option.

"Ma?" Chantelle rolled her father into the room.

Evelyn waved dismissively. "Just take his shoes off and put him in the bed. I'm about to take a bath."

She walked to the connecting bathroom and closed the door. Chantelle held her breath for fear of not holding her tongue. Her mother could be a bitch sometimes but it seemed to be the case, all the time, when it came to her pops. Oh how bad she wanted a job, a good one, so she could wheel him off and give him the life and care he deserved.

He was her motivation, the reason she'd been trying so desperately to find a job. She knew that no one took her seriously, assumed her to be an irresponsible twit, but she'd show them. Because what they didn't know was she'd been working on a master plan all along. She'd ordered a book, How to get rich in 90 days, and the ad said she'd receive it in 5 weeks or less.

Two more weeks by her count, and she'd be 90days away from going one way, to the top!

"That's right, daddy." She heaved him from the wheelchair to the bed then removed his shoes and socks. "Me and you," Kissing him on the forehead.

"Straight to the top!"

She bid him goodnight then turned to walk off, when she caught a glimpse of something in his wheel chair. On the seat, sitting flush against the side panels that held the arm rest.

Grabbing the brand new pad she turned the screen so that it faced her. A beacon flashed, signaling zero battery. "Where did you get this?" She looked back at him.

Examining the port on the side she was sure she had a charger that would fit. Cuffing it under her arm she took it with her.

Carrying it to her room she plugged it in and smiled as the screen read, charging.

.....

Aaron sat in the lonely hotel room, staring at the wall. Legs dangling off the edge of the bed, the T.V. sat on the dresser in front of him, showing pictures with the volume off.

Too zoned out to notice he just sat there, watching the light from the screen dance on the wall.

The phone rang. Maybe it was Kaleico? But how did she know where he was at, how did she find out?

"Hello."

"Sir." The female voice said. "We're getting complaints of loud music coming from your room. Could you please turn it down?"

Looking around the empty room he knew the front desk had to have called the wrong person, obviously a misunderstanding.

A frown on his face he replied. "Yeah. Sure thing." Then hung up.

Plopping back on the bed he kicked his shoes off. His flight wouldn't leave until tomorrow. All he could do was wait. He lay there wishing he'd never come in the first place. At least then he and Kaleico would still be together. Instead of being in the same city, a million miles apart.

·····

Chavis stood in the doorway of his bedroom. Directly in front of him, several feet away, the open bedroom window welcomed the winter chill. The room was frigid enough to make smoke come from his mouth when he exhaled. Stretching his hands towards the pull-up bar mounted above his head, in the doorframe, he kept his eyes locked on the window, opposite his backyard.

Wrapping his fingers around the bar he pulled, lifting himself, tilting his head forward so the bar tapped his shoulder blades with each rep. The cold air evaporating the sweat as quick as it formed on his shirtless frame.

·····

Far away on the other end of the desolate lawn, sitting in the dark confines of her bedroom, Zayeda activating a night vision App on her phone held the device up and zoomed in. Watching Chavis rise, fall and rise, pulling, lowering and pulling himself up, over and over again.

The phone trembled in her hand as she tried to hold it upright. Suddenly he dropped down. Walking towards the window he stood there for a moment, watching. But she knew he couldn't see her.

Could he?

After a few seconds he took a few steps back. Peeling off his shorts he now stood completely naked. Stepping back towards the window his eyes seemed to peer at her knowingly. Gazing at her, two shiny beady lights illuminated on the green tinted screen, looking at her as he took his staff in his palm and began to prime it, so that it enlarged on her screen. Then he indiscreetly began to pleasure himself.

.....

Downstairs Kaleico lay asleep on the couch, eyes dancing behind closed lids. Next to her lay opened photo albums filled with pictures of family and friends. Right beside her head a very old picture, she was six years old, dressed in a princess costume being carried by her dad.

Remnants of a past that leapt from the pages of the album, landing in the depths of her subconscious, fueling her dreams.

"Daddy?" There she was a young teen, standing by her bedroom window.

Looking out at the swimming pool admiring its sun glazed electric blue color, the smile on her face disappearing when, on the other side of the pool, she saw her father dangling from the fence.

Running down the stairs, her legs moving like quicksand was beneath them, it took all of her strength just to get to the door leading out back.

"Daddy." He kicked and gurgled as the rope tightened around his neck.

Just over his head slightly above the fence a tree house hovered. Anchored by a tree in their neighbors, Chavis' yard on the opposite side of the fence, hanging over their side like a decorative awning.

"Daddy!"

She ran screaming all the way to the pools edge. Her father at the other end convulsing, life seeping from him with each passing second she stepped out into the water, only to find that it merely rippled beneath her feet, but did not break and envelope her.

She began to walk across the water with little to no effect at all. Trasping across it like a dragon fly on the hunt, she quickly found her way to the other end.

"Daddy!" She cried. Grabbing his feet she began to push upward.

She barely had the strength to lift them. He was far heavier than anything she'd ever attempted to lift in her life.

Her father's eyes began to bulge. Leg's kicking till she was knocked aside, left to lay on the ground, looking up at him as the rope around his neck slowly began to claim his life.

"Daddy!" She screamed. "I'm sorry, daddy. Daddy I'm sorry! Please forgive me. Please daddy. Please forgive me, please!"

Her tears met the ground and began to trickle down the cement, rolling off into the swimming pool. The more she cried for her father, the more the tears streamed into the pool causing the water to rise till it spilled above the rim, and began to wash her way. Before long she could feel it's moisture creeping up the inside of her legs.

"Daddy! Daddy!"

"Daddy!" she jerked from sleep, still crying aloud. "I'm sorry daddy. Please please.. I .."

She stopped. Realizing she'd been dreaming. A dream that was all too real. So real that she could still feel herself getting wet.

"Dammit!" She looked down at herself.

The couch was damp and her pajamas were drenched with piss. This never ceased to anger her. Though it'd happened many times before, the dreams and the resulting inability to hold her bladder, were always something she could never get used to.

Getting up from the couch she sat the albums on the floor. Removing her pants, using them to wipe at her thighs, she took her panties off and bawled them up in the wet pajama bottoms.

Letting her Tee-shirt do it's best to cover her exposed portions, Kaleico unzipped the couch cushions and took the covers off. Walking commando to the laundry room she dumped everything in the washer before running up the stairs to get herself cleaned up.

·····

Chapter 28

Chantelle was almost asleep when a light bump made her open her eyes. Another bump. Bump. Bump.

"ILK!" She gasped. Hearing her mother's moans before the headboard bumped and thudded once more.

She couldn't imagine how Evelyn could find so many ways to thrill herself in a room, with no one but a paraplegic for company. Truth was she didn't want to imagine it. In fact she hated the rare occasions when she'd hear such moans oozing through the walls.

Getting up to grab her headphones from the dresser she noticed the I-pad from her father's wheelchair was now fully charged. Picking it up she turned it on and her eyes grew the size of marbles, when she read the words printed across the screen.

The words were her father's. A message, unknown to her, that was typed while he sat in a room earlier with Aaron, learning how to use the device. A message interrupted by the subject of the message. Words typed for Aaron by her dad that Aaron never got to read.

CHAVIS DID THIS TO ME CHAVIS DID THIS TO ME cHaVIS did this to me chavis chavis chavis did this

"What?" Chantelle began to shake.

What was this? Some sort of a joke? It had to be a joke, right? The music played in her ears as she cupped the pad in her palm and went to ask her father what this was. What it meant.

Her thoughts distorted and ears distracted she'd forgotten about her mother, and when she began to open their bedroom door, what she saw quickly made her pull it back to a close.

It was her mother. Evelyn straddling her father's face, bucking and rolling her hips, without much notice of her daughter's entrance or exit.

Disgusted, Chantelle ran down the hall. Still in her pajamas' grabbing the keys to the van, slipping her bunny slippers on, she ran out of the house.

Dialing Chavis' number as she drove, she failed to get an answer. Fine. He'd have no choice but to answer soon enough.

Chapter 29

After spending time in the shower Kaleico felt refreshed. Stepping out she realized she'd failed to bring a towel. Brushing the droplets away with her palms, stepping out into the hallway, beads of water stained the carpet as she walked towards the linen closet.

She noticed the door to her old room was open a crack. A strange glow coming from the narrow opening caught her eye. Pausing to peek inside Kaleico saw her sister, sitting with her back turned to her. Feet propped up on the window sill, the iridescent green glow around her head made Zayeda look like she was in line for an alien abduction.

Kaleico was about to announce herself, about to ask if she was alright, when she figured out the source of the green hue was the phone Zayeda held in her grips, holding it slightly above eye level, pointing it at the window.

Staying quiet and out of sight Kaleico cocked her head and squinted, brow furrowing when she realized the green light was a night vision setting. Then what she saw on the screen made her gasp.

It was Chavis, plain as day, standing in the window across the lawn, stark naked, fondling himself while Zayeda sat there in a trance watching him.

Forgetting about a towel Kaleico stepped away from the door. Fist clenched, fleeting down the stairs, stopping by the room formerly occupied by Aaron she grabbed a pair of sweats and a Tee he'd left behind, before throwing on a pair of old sneakers from the closet and storming out of the door.

"You filthy, no good ... wait till I get my hands on you!" Stepping out into the cold frost covered grass, running towards the back of the house, she stopped.

Thinking better of it. She didn't want Chavis or Zayeda to see her crossing the lawn. Making a U-turn Kaleico decided to take the long way around. Hitting the street she took off, heading around the corner, running towards the next block, where she would confront Chavis face to face in his own home.

Chapter 30

Aaron had barely slept more than a wink. The T.V. signaled that the satellite link was being disrupted. He flipped the channels with no luck. There was nothing but a blue screen to greet him with the same message at each station selected.

Tossing the remote he got up and peered out the hotel window. "No wonder!"

Kaleico had always told him there wasn't much snowfall in Charlotte, but the wee hours of Christmas Eve, turned Christmas, begged to differ. It wasn't much, barely sprinkling the ground as it made contact, it seemed to form traces of light slush in portions of the parking lot that were covered by water.

Giving up on sleep he looked at the clock. 3:40 a.m. Still hours from his trip to the airport he scratched his head, deciding if he couldn't sleep he need something else to pass the time.

Picking up his phone he was about to fumble with an online game app, when he remembered something. Uncle Melvin. He never finished showing him the full application of the program. He'd also failed to even mention it to his caregivers, Evelyn or Chantelle, giving them any idea of how it worked.

"I know what I can do."

He could access it from his phone and set up an opening message, and instructional piece that would display once the device was turned on.

He talked to himself as he tapped at the screen, accessing the device. Upon opening it, he stumbled upon the previously recorded work, from Melvin's attempts to work it earlier.

He smiled as he read the first letters. The letters he'd struggled to manipulate with a wink and movement of the eye, a C then a H then ...

He scrolled the phone down, tilting it sideways, expanding the screen he couldn't believe what he was reading. Melvin must have typed it when Chavis had interrupted them earlier that night.

A message he never got to see, until now.

CHAVIS DID THIS TO ME. Chavis. Chavis. Chavis.

A repetitive rant, a declaration that made his heart sink.

"What?" What did he mean, Chavis did this to me? What else could he possibly mean? "But .. why would he say .."

Suddenly the blue screen on the T.V. snapped back to life. It was on the news. A familiar broadcast. He'd seen this before.

"Police still have no leads on the death of a young employee a few nights ago ..."

An officer in charge popped up on the screen. "All we have is a blurry image picked up from one of the nearby cameras of an adjacent parking lot. Unfortunately the distorted video is hard to see." They flashed the image.

Aaron eased close to the screen.

"That looks like."

The news report continued. *"Police say there's not much additional evidence"* They showed the crime scene again "If anyone has any information to share you can call …"

Then Aaron saw it. One of the officers in the background walked towards the Crime lab van with something in his hand. A clear bag, an evidence bag, and though it was off in the distance Aaron's eyes couldn't miss its contents. A bright green and purple scarf. A scarf he'd seen at that very bar. Worn by

"Chavis."

In a state of sudden panic he began to dial Kaleico's number. There was no answer. He called again. Nothing.

With no time to waste he left the motel room behind. Waiting for a cab was not an option. Aaron took off running as fast as he could, heading back to Kaleico's mother's house.

·····

Chapter 31

The only time Melvin's slobbering didn't irritate Evelyn were times like now. His salivating lips, playing slip and slide for her open, crotch made her squeal and shudder. The bump, bump, bump of the headboard against the bedroom wall a perfect beat, on sync with the bumping of her clitoris against the tip of his huge prominent nose.

Bump. Bump. Bump. Bump. Bump.

.....

Chavis stepped away from the window, a hard knock at the front door called for investigation. Grabbing his boxers he pulled them on and ran out into the hall, stopping at the top of the stairs. Before he could get down them, the front door flung open. He froze.

Chantelle crossed the threshold "You son of a bitch!" She yelled, arms flailing in anger as she ran up the steps.

·····

Like thunderous footsteps in the wake of giants, the headboard rocked and banged, echoing in Evelyn's mind, eyes aflutter as she imagined it was Chavis' face nestled in her thighs.

But it was the vibration from Melvin's expelled breath, spent from trapped nostrils begging for air that sent her neck into a hair whipping whirl, till she began to grow dizzy and see stars.

Then she realized. The tiny little dots that danced around in her line of sight weren't stars at all.

It was something she'd seen in her peripheral while her head was spinning. Something outside her bedroom window.

Snowfall.

·····

Kaleico rounded the block. Flecks of snow came from the sky, tapping her temple and parts of her arm as she made her way to Chavis' drive. The road was taking on light slush and she could feel the moisture, dampening her feet.

Distracted by the soiled sneakers she didn't notice at first, but then she looked up. "What the .."

Why was Evelyn's van parked out front? Picking up her pace, a scream met her ears as she got closer to the house.

"No..NO..No." Kaleico panicked as she reached the porch and tried to turn the doorknob.

The door was locked. She remembered the spare key under the mat, Chavis left it there for emergencies. Everyone in her family knew about this key, just as Chavis knew about the spare kept at Sandra's house.

The key was gone. Another shriek followed by a loud thud made her run to the nearest window. Peering inside she could see shadows on the floor, cast from upstairs, dancing about. That's when she realized the window was unlocked. Pressing her palms against the pane she was able to push it up just enough to slip her fingers beneath it, and open it completely.

Climbing inside, crawling to her feet, Kaleico spotted Chavis, upstairs leaning against the railing. But between the railing and himself Chantelle stood wedged and helpless, gagging, struggling to tear his hands from her throat.

Still clutching the I-pad she swung it as hard as she could smashing him in the face, doing nothing to free his grip it bounced off and tumbled over the rail.

Kaleico stood below yelling up at him. "Chavis, stop!"

The pad came tumbling from above, landing at her feet. The screen facing up. CHAVIS DID THIS TO ME was all she saw.

"Chavis No! Stop!"

Kaleico's legs felt as if they were cemented to the floor, motionless as her cousin convulsed overhead, gurgling as the railing began to creak until it turned into a loud cracking sound.

. . . . .

Evelyn screamed aloud. The headboard creaking and popping as she pulled it towards her, pushing her hips forward so that Melvin's drooling mouth drenched her from cunt to taint. While she in turn began to drench his entire face

"Oooh Oooh Ohhhh!"

.....

Clank .Clank. Crack. The old railing above snapped raining debris down upon Kaleico who gained control of her legs, just in time to leap out of the way.

.....

"God! That was good!" Evelyn rolled to her side of the bed. Reaching over to caress her husband's face. "Wha ... Melvin? Melvin!" She raised up on her elbow. "Melvin!" Calling his name again "Melvin!"

And the reality hit.

"No! God please ... God please! God please!"

.....

Kaleico lay on the floor amidst the fallen debris- screws and bits of wood railing. Her eyes teared up as she looked at the vacant stare on her cousin's face. Chantelle lay on the floor, right next to her, with blood trickling from her ear and mouth. Hands trembling and twitching as her lashes began to flutter about.

Chavis stared down from what remained of the broken rail. Using his forearm to wipe at his bloody mouth he wiped his hands on his boxers, looking down at Kaleico he began to slowly descend the stairs.

Glaring at him as he reached the bottom and took steps towards her, Kaleico took the I-pad from the floor, flinging it at him as she cursed.

"What have you done, you son of a bitch! What have you done!"

Deflecting the device he closed in in her, wrapping his arms around her, pulling her close to his chest.

Chapter 32

Aaron left a trail of steam behind him, nostrils puffing spent air into the cold as he came within close proximity of Kaleico's home.

Disoriented he'd mistakenly taken the route that lead to Chavis' street, instead of Kaleico's. The error came to light when he saw Chavis home come into view.

Deciding his best plan of action would be to cut through the yard, he began to veer off, Evelyn's van didn't go without notice. *Chavis did this to me.* The message ran through his mind. The irony, Melvin's wife at her gentleman caller's house the same night the truth came to light.

Cutting through the yard Aaron heard a scream. Stopping in his tracks he back pedaled.

That scream. The voice. Kaleico.

"Kaleico!" He ran to the front door. "Kaleico!"

Something in the window made him stop. He saw Kaleico crying out as Chavis advanced on her, grabbing her in his arms.

Taking a running start Aaron burst through the door. Running straight into Chavis till they both stumbled and fell to the floor, tripping over what Aaron realized was, "A person?"

"Chantelle? Chantelle!" He scrambled to a crawl.

Checking her pulse, when suddenly a hard blow to the back of the head knocked him unconscious.

Chapter 33

Aaron's head throbbed, vision blurry at best as he began to make out figures in the room. A bed sat nearby. On it lay Chantelle. Next to her sitting on its edge was Kaleico, a bloody towel in hand, she dabbed desperately at Chantelle's head.

"Chavis." Kaleico called out making Aaron look to his left, where Chavis stood staring at the wall. "She's not responding. She won't stop bleeding. We have to do something!" She cried. "She's gonna die. Oh God please don't let her die."

Aaron's mouth was like cotton. "Kaleico."

He didn't understand. Why were they in a bedroom. How had they moved. How did

Chantelle end up on a bed, and why .. Why hadn't Kaleico called for help?

Chavis turned and walked towards the bed.

Aaron lurched forward. "Get away from her you ..." Realizing for the first time his hands were binded. So were his legs. Both tied to an old rickety chair.

He struggled. This caused the chair to grind and scrape at the floor, which made Chavis redirect focus. Changing course Chavis darted towards Aaron delivering a hard backhand to his face.

Aarons head lobbed. Blood spilling from his mouth as Kaleico jumped up, shoving Chavis aside.

"No!" She shook a finger at him. "No Chavis. No more.!"

Chavis lowered his head like a disobedient pup, and walked back to the corner where he just stood, starring at the wall.

Kaleico spoke to Chavis as she turned to face Aaron. "Just.." She paused, flipping her hair. "Everybody just woosah.. caalm down."

Aaron's teeth were stained with blood. "Wha..I don't.. what the fuck is this?"

Resting a hand on his knee as she squat down in front of him. "Shhh..Shhhushh." trying to soothe him. "Just calm down. Calm down, we can fix this." Turning to look at her cousin, unconscious on the bed then Chavis standing by the wall, then back to Aaron. "Yeah. Yeah. We can fix..."

"What the fuck do you mean, fix it?" Aaron made the chair hop as he tried to break free.

"Aaron baby just, just shhh.. It's gonna be okay" she cupped his face and began to spread kisses about it." Just calm down, sweety."

He began to calm down.

"That's momma's big man." She coaxed.

He looked at her confused. He didn't understand.

Brushing her hair from her face she stood and began to pace. "Okay. Okay." Facing Aaron she snapped her fingers. "This is what happened!"

Chavis' voice boomed from the corner. "He's gonna tell the cops!" he turned. "Can't you see? Why?..why is he so special?"

"Chavis" She demanded. "Calm down!"

"No! I won't!" He punched the wall. "No! I've done everything you asked of me. All these years. All of that, and you still treat me like .. like I'm not ..." he charged towards Aaron. "What makes him better than me!"

"Stop!" She stood in front of him, blocking his path, staring him down.

He stopped. Heaving as he continued. "Everything you ever asked me to do, I did it. Everything!" he glared back at her. "Your Uncle ... your father."

"Her.. her father?" Aaron uttered, no one heard him.

Kaleico was unresponsive. Standing there in a trance, when suddenly the floor beneath her feet seemed to change in appearance, taking on the form of rippling water, the face that stared back at her from the electric blue surface was her own. A reflection of the past.

Chapter 34

For as long as she could remember, Kaleico had a hold on Chavis, though exactly when it all started she was not sure?

There was the time, when they were kids. They sat in the back yard playing, Kaleico with her favorite doll, Chavis with his favorite action figure. They were enjoying themselves playing a game of tie the knot with their toy counterparts, having a mock wedding in their honor.

"You may now kiss the bride." Kaleico played priest.

Mashing the doll's faces together they sealed the deal and all was joyous. That is until Kaleico leaned forward and planted one on his action figure's cheek.

She still could remember clear as day. Him getting angry, ripping the arms and legs off his toy soldier, biting the head off. Chewing it to bits and spitting it out, before burying every bit and piece in her backyard. Making her newlywed doll a widow, all in one instance.

Then there was that time she'd gotten that fluffy white puppy. Pepper she'd named it. But she barely paid Chavis any attention whenever he and the dog were in the same vicinity, Pepper was soft and fluffy. The only thing she seemed to get more joy from was watching Chavis seethe whenever she nestled the fluffy dog against her cheek.

"What's wrong?" She'd asked him one day, right before giving the dog a smooch. "You jealous?"

Her father had apologized a million times over, after rolling over the poor little puppy, while on his riding mower. "I didn't see him run around the corner!" her father had cried, as chunks of the mangled dog lay scattered by the mowers blade. "It's like it came outta nowhere."

But how could he have seen it? How could he have known that on that day Chavis had snatched the dog from her grip, and rolled it like a bowling ball, just as her father made the corner, making it desert for the large mower.

Her father had thought she was in shock because she hadn't cried. To make up, he'd bought she and Chavis ice cream. But she wasn't in shock at all. She was in awe.

And so it went. Elementary school. The little Asian boy who fell victim to the merry-go-round accident. Kaleico had called the boy her 'boyfriend', at least that's what she kept telling Chavis. "What's wrong?" She teased. "You jealous?"

He was, and using the strength of ten men he'd showed her just how jealous he could get. Grabbing the rung of the merry-go-round, after asking the boy to grab something from the ground beneath it, he sent it spinning, crashing into the boy's head, tearing a gash across his face.

The boy didn't tell. Kaleico had made sure of it. She 'fixed it." She always fixed it.

Then there was middle school. She'd intentionally lured a boy who often teased her, to the spot where she knew Chavis always hid, during class, when he didn't want to be around anyone.

Taking the unsuspecting boy there, just before she knew Chavis would arrive, letting him fondle and grope her. She hated it but when she saw Chavis coming around the corner, she pretended to like it.

"Kaleico!" Chavis said in disbelief. "What are you doing? Why are you back here?"

She'd looked him in the eyes and replied. "Why do you care?" With total disregard, she rubbed the boy's crotch.

"What's wrong? .. are you jealous or something?"

Her ogling hands made the boy look at Chavis and smile. It was the last time he'd smiled, with a full set of teeth ever again. The poor boy was sure to have told but Kaleico - fixing it- had warned, if he told she would lie to the faculty, say he'd forced her beneath the bleachers and tried to rape her.

Just like that, he kept his toothless mouth shut.

But with middle school also came the development of womanly parts. She hated the way Evelyn's husband looked at her, whenever they visited. Always wanting to hug her. Always wanting to kiss her on the cheek. Sometimes slipping closer to the lips than she liked.

She hated the way his hands felt. Didn't want him to touch her anymore. "Ever again."

And he didn't. He couldn't. It happened one summer day, when he'd come over to help Sandra with an issue with her car. Melvin lay under it, with it lifted up on a jack, fumbling away at the undercarriage.

Chavis had come out of nowhere. Melvin saw his feet as he glanced from under the car. "Chavis. Wusup my man?" he'd called out and asked. "Since you standing there, how bout giving me a wrench."

Chavis gave it to him. Right across the knee cap. Swinging it with all his might as hard and fast as he could, repeatedly beating at his knees and shins, till Melvin began to scramble about. Trying to slide from beneath the car when his leg swung too far to one side, knocking the jack off kilter.

The sound of the vehicle crushing his skull still echoed in Kaleico's head to this day. She'd stood nearby, peeking around the corner of the house, watching. She watched until he ceased to twitch and then she ran screaming to her mother and Aunt.

But when the medics arrived and said. "He's still breathing." She knew there was nothing she could do to fix it. This time Chavis would surely pay a price.

But she found out, as fate would have it, some things fix themselves. Although Melvin survived he'd been rendered immobile and unable to speak. A vegetable the doctor's had said, assuring there would never be much more to him, in the form of function, nor sensibility.

·····

The doctors were wrong. She'd seen the message he'd typed on the pad. An attempt to finger Chavis after all these years.

She'd come too far to let it all come crashing down on her now. Especially the demise of her father.

Chapter 35

At first Kaleico hadn't believed Chavis when he told her.

"Kaleico. Your dad is sleeping with my mom."

"No!" She refuted. "You're lying. Why are you lying?"

Chavis hated her father and she knew it. She knew that Chavis loved to watch her laying by the pool, lusting over her from afar.

But that was before her father had put the fence up. "I'm putting this up to keep that boy from looking at you, when you're in the pool." That's what he'd told her.

Truth was she had no objections to him watching, she made sure to give him plenty to see when no one was looking.

Her father's attempts did nothing to deter Chavis, there was still Kaleico's bedroom window. And with the help of the tree house, he'd built after the fence went up, he could see directly into it.

"The fence your father built wasn't for me." Chavis had explained. "He built it, to hide it, to keep you away from my mother's window."

His mother's window could be seen clearly from Kaleico's room. Chavis bedroom just below hers also was granted the same line of sight, til the fence came.

Unable to convince her he told her to join him in the treehouse. "Sneak out tonight. He always comes, when they think I'm asleep." He told her. "I hear them in my room. That's why I leave out. Why I go to my treehouse, so I don't have to hear."

She still didn't want to believe it, but he'd assured her.

"Tonight. I'll show you."

In hopes of proving him wrong she snuck out, seeing it with her own eyes. From high up in the treehouse her father's infidelity shone plain as day, under the moonlit sky.

"How could he?" Her mother had loved him unconditionally. How could he do this to she and her sister? Their entire family?

She hated him. Before she realized it she'd cried out in agony. Fleeing from the treehouse as her father watched.

She knew.

What could her father do, but intercept her? Cutting her off at the front of Chavis' house, he'd snatched her inside and whooped her. Disregarding his own actions he'd whooped her for being out of the house, for being nosey. Being in adults business.

Chavis had tried to stop him, but he'd pushed him down and Chavis' mother did nothing. Said nothing in his defense.

All Chavis could do was watch as Kaleico's father drug her to the car. Slapping her calm before making his way home.

The next day Kaleico was incoherent, not speaking to Chavis. Lost. Then it turned into a week. Then another. Chavis was about to give up hope, when finally she spoke.

"I wish he was dead."

Chapter 36

Aaron looked up at Kaleico, calling her name for the fourth time. "Kaleico?" She didn't respond. He called her again, this time her eyes showed presence. "Kaleico..what..what is he saying?"

Chavis interrupted. "He's gonna tell it. You know what we have to.."

"No!" She stomped her foot, pointing an index at Chavis, stabbing at the air with every word. "No! I said no! We want! We want! You hear me?"

Eye's welling up she faced Aaron again, moving closer.

"Aaron baby." She knelt in front of him, this made Chavis fume. "It was..All of what he's saying. It was just … it was necessary. It was.."

"Necessary?" Aaron made the chair shake as he spoke "Kaleico. You have to let me go. You have to untie me!"

"Baby you gotta tell me you won't tell." She tried to reason "You gotta tell me you're not.."

"Let me.." Aaron jerked his shoulders around trying to break the bindings. "Go!"

Chavis shouted. "Kaleico we gotta"

"No!" She shook her head in denial. "He won't tell. He's gonna. He loves me. Don't you baby?" She rubbed his legs. "Tell him baby." Moving close to his crotch. "Tell him, you won't tell. Tell him."

"I won't .. I" Aaron started then lost composure. "Let me go you crazy bitch!" Spittle flying from his mouth, veins rising around his temple as he began to rant."You and this crazy, sonofabitch neighbor of yours better" he made the chair hop, up and down, the legs beating on the floor, emphasizing each word. "Let me go, right fuckin now!"

Kaleico threw her forearms over her ears, ruffling her hair as she let out an ear piercing scream.

This made Aaron freeze. Chavis still in the corner perked up, fist clenched tight he began to shuffle anxiously.

Finally, her high pitched tantrum ceased. "Okay. Okay." She took a few deep breaths, inhaling, exhaling, inhaling, exhaling nice and slow. "Okay. Okay." She stood over Aaron. "It's okay. Its okay, baby. I know what I have to do. I have.. I gotta let you go. I gotta let you go."

This was music to his ears. "Yeah. That's right, baby." Aaron coaxed. "You gotta let me go."

Chavis tensed. "Kaleico"

"I gotta let him go. I gotta do it. I gotta do it." She talked to herself as she sat in Aaron's lap, cradling his face. "I'm sorry, baby. I'm so sorry." Wrapping her arms around him, she hugged him tight.

Chavis stood behind Aaron, watching as she took him in her arms. Letting her hands fall towards his binded wrist she fumbled with the rope then let her fingers interlock with his for a second. "Chavis."

She could see Chavis' knuckles turn white. He hated seeing her in his lap.

Chavis sneered through gritted teeth. "What?"

Releasing her grip. She let Aaron's fingers fall away from her own as she looked at Chavis and asked.

"Does this make you jealous?"

She tilted Aaron's head back, pressing her tongue into his mouth. His muffled protest unable to escape his lips as he tried to resist.

Chavis snapped. In one swift motion he was across the room, knocking her from Aaron's lap, wrapping her binded boyfriend in a rear neck choke, that made him gasp as Kaleico hit the floor.

Eyes wild Chavis squeezed. "It makes me jealous!" Squeezing harder. "very jealous!"

Kaleico lay on the floor looking up at them. Aaron's eyes bulging, nostrils spilling snot as he struggled for air.

And in that moment, once again, she saw her father.

Chapter 37

Chavis had planned it to a tee. But there was only one thing he'd miscalculated. This he found out the hard way.

Sitting high up in the treehouse, watching. Waiting. It was early morning, Kaleico's father always cleaned the pool this time of day.

When he arrived, Chavis watched him use the long handled net to scoop fallen leaves and lingering insects from the water. Waiting for him to get close enough.

Rounding the side of the pool close to the fence he didn't bother to look up at the treehouse overhead. Didn't see the rope slithering down like a snake ready to strike.

Caught off guard, the slipknot fell over his head, and immediately began to tighten.

The clang of the pool net made Kaleico, lying in bed, jump to attention. When she got up to investigate she was shocked to see her father struggling, his back against the fence; above him Chavis in the treehouse, pulling a length of rope.

That's when she jumped up and ran down the stairs.

Chavis had managed to catch his neck. Jumping from the treehouse descending on his own yard, he let the rope fall over a limb. Riding it on the way down so that it yanked her father, on the opposite side of the fence, up onto his toes.

Chavis landed on the ground and slid slightly. He didn't weigh enough. Her father's weight made the limb warp and spring upward. The recoil yanking Chavis back, lifting him so that it left both he and her father with nothing but tip toes on the ground.

Kaleico came running, alongside the edge of the pool. Her father's toes scraping the ground she could see the relief in his eyes, when she ran over and grabbed his feet, pushing upward.

The pressure on his neck slacked a bit, but the look of relief suddenly changed when he heard her say one single word.

. . . . .

Chavis suddenly felt the rope slack on his his end. His feet found the ground and a voice from the other side of the fence began to shout.

"Pull. Pull. Pull!"

Chapter 38

Aaron looked exactly like her father had. Legs kicking, face puffing as Chavis extracted life with each passing second. His skin turned flush then purple all in one instance. Until finally, just like it had come with her father, a gurgle emitted then he ceased to move.

.....

"He's dead."

Evelyn sat on her porch, eyes flooded with tears as the paramedic put a hand on her shoulder and spoke again.

"Mam?" He knelt beside her. "Did you hear me?" he reiterated. "We did all we could do but,"

"I heard." She sobbed. "Dead. He's dead … Oh my God, he's dead."

And she had killed him. Smothered him with her own retched cunt. Now she felt guilty for the fact, her only thought, while riding his face had been,

"I wish he'd just die."

Die. So that she could move on with life. She was tired of wheeling him around. Tired of being with a man who couldn't please her. Tired of not being able to spend every moment of her life with the man she truly wanted. She was free.

Looking at the paramedic she then looked around, confused.

"My … my van? Where's my van?"

Chapter 39

Three Months Later

Chantelle sat away from the others. Her eyes fixed on the large veranda that extended the portion of the backyard that once, long ago housed the swimming pool that she and Kaleico spent so much time in, swimming together, as kids.

But the pool was long gone. Filled in by Chavis. Just as the fence that once separated her Aunt Sandra's yard from Chavis' home was now gone. More of his work. Like the new addition to Sandra's home, the veranda. Not only Chavis' idea but an accredit to his handiwork.

Cutting her eyes towards the house she could see through the kitchen window's parted curtains, stealing a glance at Chavis, as he assisted Sandra with something. But not before having a wet kiss sneaked to him, after the two of them made sure no one was looking. Though it was clear they weren't worried about her wandering eyes.

Perhaps her Aunt's affection was just thanks for his handi-work. Chantelle was sure, from the looks of the exchange, his handi-work extended far beyond the pool, the fence or the new porch in the back.

The porch was now donned with long lengths of ribbons and balloons that danced in the wind, as joyous and lively as those whom occupied the long table in the center of the porch.

Kaleico sat with her back to Chantelle. In front of her, Zayeda sat off to the side a bit so that Chantelle had a clear view of her face. She looked happy. But weren't all girls on their 18th Birthday.

"Happy Biiirthdaay tooo yooou.." Sandra began as she followed Chavis out the door, stepping out onto the porch. The two of them smiling and singing cheerfully.

Kaleico at the table joined in as Zayeda blushed and grinned from ear to ear.

So young and innocent. Chantelle thought to herself. Zayeda had no clue what sort of horrors the world held. Horrors that she needed to go no further than where she sat, to find herself in the midst of.

Chantelle couldn't help but wonder. Would the young innocent girl be smiling so hard if she knew the platform for her birthday party, the veranda, was no more than a large lid, designed to make sure Chavis' secrets stayed buried.

All assumptions on Chantelle's part, but an assumption that she was willing to bet her life on.

She'd heard mention of Aaron here and there. Questions asked by Sandra that got shrugged off, or brushed under the rug. Kaleico had moved on. That was the just of it.

Look at them. All one big happy family.

All they were missing was.

"Evelyn!" Sandra called out.

"Finally." Chantelle thought as her mother came around the corner. She'd forgotten something in the van, ran back to get it while Chantelle waited patiently. But what choice did she have these days. Patience was much more than a virtue.

Chavis looked when Sandra called out to her sister.

Sandra continued. "I didn't hear yall pull up. You should've honked the horn. I would've helped."

Sandra took a step towards them but Chavis stopped her. "I got her, Sandra. Go ahead and enjoy the cake." He jumped off the porch. "I'll take care of it."

Sandra thanked him. Taking a seat she and Kaleico shared their thoughts on the cake as Zayeda began to blow out the candles.

Chavis came to a halt, just in front of Chantelle and Evelyn. "I got her." He smiled.

Evelyn smiled back. Whispering as she passed. "You got anything planned for tonight?"

"We'll see." He replied "We'll see."

He snuck a slap to her ass, sending her towards the veranda.

Then he knelt down in front of Chantelle and whispered. "You understand that I never wanted this?" he gestured towards her legs.

Standing upright he got behind her and began to push the wheelchair towards the veranda. He'd just added the wheelchair access ramp, per Sandra's request.

Chantelle wanted nothing more than to lift her hand, raise her middle finger and tell him to go fuck himself. But it was useless, she couldn't.

How had she come to this? Her mind only held flashes from that night. She and Chavis fighting. Falling off the stairs. Kaleico was there. Aaron, she'd seen him, too. Seen Kaleico crying. Heard something about a shovel. Next thing she knew she'd blacked out completely. Coming to, in a hospital bed.

Black ice. That's what the police report said. They'd found her behind the wheel of the van once used to haul her dad around. It was wrapped around a pole. How she'd lived was a mystery.

She was sure it hadn't been Chavis' intention for her to survive. But she'd never be the same. She now knew her father's pain, firsthand.

Chavis pushed her next to Kaleico and Sandra. Tears welled in Chantelle's eyes as Kaleico looked at her and smiled. Coddling her like a child as she quipped. "Hey cous!"

Chavis took a seat on the other side, between Zayeda and Evelyn. He wished Zayeda a happy birthday.

Her hand beneath the table, on his knee, sliding towards his crotch. Tonight was her night. She was 18 now. He had promised.

But not if Evelyn had her way. Her hand caressing his lower back, as she anticipated him inside her, tonight.

Kaleico looked at him and smiled. 'He'll always be mine.' She thought as she turned to wipe a bit of drool from Chantelle's mouth. 'Always.'

Chantelle's cheek became tear stained. Her body trembling as she began to grunt, unable to form words, she screamed on the inside.

CHAVIS DID THIS TO ME. Chavis did this to me. Chavis. Chavis, Chavis!

FRIEND OF THE FAMILY

G. legacy